Scrooge Me Again

Paranormal Dating Agency Holidays

USA Today & *New York Times*
Bestselling Author

MILLY TAIDEN

This book is a work of fiction. The names, characters, places, and incidents are fictitious or have been used fictitiously, and are not to be construed as real in any way. Any resemblance to persons, living or dead, actual events, locales, or organizations is entirely coincidental.

Published By
Latin Goddess Press, Inc.
Winter Springs, FL 32708
http://millytaiden.com
Scrooge Me Again
Copyright © 2018 by Milly Taiden
Cover by: Willsin Rowe
Edited by: Tina Winograd

All Rights Are Reserved. No part of this book may be used or reproduced in any manner whatsoever without written permission, except in the case of brief quotations embodied in critical articles and reviews.
Property of Milly Taiden
December 2018

SCROOGE ME AGAIN

Zaria Grande can't believe she's invited to a royal birthday party...on another planet and accompanied by a matchmaker! The friend who invited her is clearly nuts. Another planet, hah! But...what if she begs this matchmaker to hook her up? It's about time she found a strapping hot shifter to cuddle with this Christmas. As long as he's no Scrooge, she's open to anything.

Jaded by the Earthling's materialistic mentality during the holidays, Quint Treyvaal doesn't care much for parties and socializing. But he wants a mate. He asked Gerri to find him a female and she delivers a few hours later. Talk about express service! Losing his mate the next day isn't part of the plan. Time to show Zaria this lion's the only man for her.

Quint's hard work to romance Zaria is put to the test when a wrench is thrown into his plans. For Zaria, leaving her life on Earth might be asking too much. Quint's going to need extra help to get his mate to see that loving him is a chance worth taking.

ATTENTION READERS:

This is a holiday novella. While it can be read as a standalone full-length story like the other PDA books, I recommend reading the other Nova Aurora PDA books to get to know other characters and enjoy their stories as well. Enjoy.

—For everyone who loves a holiday romance. Get you a sexy shifter to keep you warm!

PROLOGUE

You are cordially invited to a most festive celebration! Please help us celebrate Avery, Aahron and Aden's 2nd birthdays.

Gerri set the invitation on her desk and opened the letter from Bella next.

Dear Gerri,

As you may have seen the triplets are turning two and we would love for you to come celebrate with us. Their birthday happens to be on the same day as a good friend of mine, who I haven't seen since coming to Aurora. I was hoping you could escort her here for the party. With your permission, I will have her meet you at your apartment on the day of the party. Her name is Zaria and I know you will get along fantastically.

All my love
Bella

Gerri sat back at her desk and smiled, a visit to Aurora sounded exactly like what she needed right now. The lovely warmth of Aurora would be welcomed now that there was a snow storm coming up. She'd be back in time for the holidays and her annual charity ball. Besides, there were always a few stray cats who needed a hand finding their mate and she was between clients at the moment anyway. She pulled out her communicator and replied right away to Bella.

ONE

Zaria Grande stared at the letter in her hand. What the hell? She hadn't heard from Bella in a long time. All her emails went unanswered and her letters never got replies. Now, out of the blue, she received a letter inviting her to Aurora to celebrate her triplets', yes, triplets' birthday. She frowned. She hadn't even known Bella was married, let alone had three kids.

Wait, the crazy didn't end there. She asked her to meet some strange woman at an address she'd never been to, which was the first way to get yourself killed. But then, this stranger was going to take her through a portal to another planet.

She'd known Bella in high school and college

and there was no way she'd written that letter. Except, she'd said personal things. Things only Bella knew of Zaria.

There was only one conclusion. This was obviously evidence that Bella was off her rocker. She shook her head. Dear god, her friend had lost her marbles. Magical portal and other planets, that was crazy. That was all well and good, so why was she standing outside Gerri Wilder's apartment door getting ready to knock?

Because, Zaria sighed, on the off chance there was more out there, her adventurous soul demanded she take this step. If there were other planets and species and somehow Bella had been able to discover something most humans could only dream of, could she say no to exploring another planet? No. So call her crazy, too, but she was ready to either be let down or meet a brand-new challenge head-on. She squared her shoulders and knocked.

Her whole body tensed as she waited for the door to open. Holy fuck. She bit her lip and waited for Gerri Wilder. Zaria wasn't stupid, she asked around and did some research about this woman. Who could've known there was a Paranormal Dating Agency and someone who actually hooked up shifters and humans? This was an idea she could get behind, fierce, sexy alpha male loving her. Hell yeah, sign her up!

"Well if that isn't a smile of a woman imagining a good O, I don't know what is." Zaria's head jerked up, she hadn't realized the door opened. Standing in front of her was a gorgeous older woman with the most beautiful eyes. Well, those weren't natural. Were her eyes an indicator she was a shifter? *And what did she say to me?* Zaria realized she was standing there with her mouth hanging open.

"Mrs. Wilder?" *There,* Zaria thought, *I can be coherent.*

"Yes, dear, come on in, but call me Gerri, please. I'm very happy you're here, we have some time before we need to leave so let's chat for a few minutes." Gerri stepped back and waved her arm at the couch in her living room. "Leave that carry-on by the door. We'll grab it on our way back out. Have a seat, and help yourself to a cookie, I have quite the sweet tooth."

Zaria was now sure she'd walked into an alternate reality. Sweet old ladies who baked didn't talk about orgasms. She must have misheard her. Yes. Lovely older women with amazing outfits and heels she'd kill for did not talk sex. Nope. With that cleared up in her mind, Zaria sat down on the couch and smiled at the sweet lady. "Thank you for agreeing to take me to Aurora. I've missed Bella like crazy and can't wait to see her again. None of my emails ever get answered and my letters don't get returned either."

"You're very welcome. And really, it's my pleasure. It's hard for Bella to communicate to anyone on this planet unless she sends someone or contacts me but she tries hard not to bother. I'm sure you know it's the children's second birthday so it should be fun. I bet Alyx must've invited half his kingdom to come to celebrate."

Zaria straightened on the couch, the cookie bite making her choke. "I'm sorry, did you say half his kingdom?"

Gerri nodded. "Give me a quick second. I need to change into something more comfortable for travel. Please, keep speaking, I'm gonna be but a second."

Zaria eyed the cookies and growled, picking up another. Damn her weakness to baked goods. She thought about Bella's letter. She had not mentioned a king. There was no way she missed that part in the letter. Bella had some explaining to do when she got there. "How did Bella meet a king?"

Gerri laughed at Zaria's shock. "I introduced them of course."

"You mean he's a shifter king? How do I get a one?" She laughed and couldn't decide if it was truly funny or if hysteria was setting in. A bite of cookie would help.

"That can be arranged," Gerri said, returning to the living room in a comfortable sweat suit with some trainers. She sat down across from Zaria. "I'm afraid it wouldn't be a king since there is only one, but a shifter of your own." Gerri leaned forward and nudged the plate of cookies to Zaria, "Eat one, the sugar will help on our trip. But first, we must see the *mane* attraction."

Eat one? She was on her third already. Ah, fuck it. She picked up another cookie. Anxiety eating was her biggest problem. "Hmm mmm, I have a feeling this is going to be a very interesting trip. Should I warn you I am allergic to dogs?"

Gerri narrowed her eyes at Zaria "There are no dog-shifters on Aurora. We do have wolves, though, but no, that is not what I have in mind for you."

Shit, I offended her. "I'm sorry, I was only teasing. You don't have to find me a date, wolf or not."

Gerri stood up and walked toward the door. "Already done, don't worry, dear. Are you ready to see Bella now?"

Zaria jumped up and followed Gerri out the door, grabbing her carry-on from the entrance. At least Bella had told her what kind of stuff to pack.

What did Gerri mean already done?

TWO

Quint Treyvaal walked into the castle and headed straight for the nursery where Avery, Aahron, and Aden spent a good portion of their time. Alyx and Bella could usually be found there spoiling the kids. Today was no exception, Quint knocked on the door and entered. Aahron gave a yell and came running over, Quint bent down and scooped him up. "Hey, cub, I missed you." He gave him a kiss on the cheek and reached down to scoop up Aden. "I couldn't forget you." The boys squealed in laughter and wiggled.

"Quint, you're looking for a quick and harsh death sentence."

Quint laughed at Alyx's concern. "What are you talking about?"

"Please put my sons down before they wiggle out of your arms again. Bella will skin you like she is always threatening if you drop one of them." Alyx laughed at the look on Quint's face. "Yes, she is standing behind you right now." Quint slowly set the boys down and turned around.

"Hi, Bella, boys are good, I promise." He backed away laughing with his hands up. "Where is my princess, Avery?"

"Quint," Bella raised an arched brow, "I keep telling Alyx a lion rug would deter any enemies. Would you like to help me test that theory?" Bella crossed her arms over her chest and glared at him.

"No, you win. I'll be careful with the precious cargo." Quint knew better than to get between a lioness and her cubs. "Let me get my kiss from Avery and I will go check on the party setup."

Alyx laughed off to his right "Smart move, I will go with you, though. Did you come over to tease Bella or did you need something before the party tonight?"

Quint spotted Avery hiding behind a couch and tiptoed over to her. "Ah, look what I found! A princess and I have rescued her!" He leaned down and scooped her up, "A knight deserves a kiss after rescuing the fair princess." He kissed her on both cheeks until she laughed and he sat her down. "Now to answer your question, I wanted to speak with you before the party."

Quint walked toward the door and stopped by Bella, "Thank you for not skinning me alive, I promise to return Alyx shortly to you."

"And then you and I," Alyx turned back to his wife and grinned at her, "have some stuff to discuss."

Bella did a mock eye-roll and burst into giggles, her face flushing as he leaned close. "I know what you want to discuss, you pervert."

"You say the sexiest things," Alyx laughed.

Quint watched Alyx kiss Bella as they left. He loved that easy humor between the couple. Not to mention that powerful connection they had. That was love. No question about it. He wanted that so badly.

"I heard a rumor that Gerri Wilder would be here tonight," Quint said, getting right to the heart of the matter. He needed that matchmaker.

"Bella invited her and asked her to bring a friend to Aurora. She should be here anytime actually. Would you like to accompany me to see if they arrived?"

The sooner Quint found Gerri, the faster he could ask for her help finding his mate. "Please, I would like to put in my request before anyone else shows up. Her services are always in demand and especially on Aurora."

"Excuse me, Sire. Mrs. Wilder and your other guest have arrived. Gerri would like to speak with you in the library if you are willing." Alyx nodded his head and continued walking.

"That was easier than I thought, let's go meet Gerri, it's funny but she specifically told me to make sure you were here tonight." Alyx laughed and clapped Quint on the shoulder. "It's about time you settled down, cousin. I can't wait to see who Gerri finds for you."

When they reached the library, Alyx opened the door and gestured Quint to enter ahead of him. "Why do I feel like you just shoved me into the Lion's Den, metaphorically speaking?"

"Wouldn't that be the Wolf's Den since I am the one you are coming to see?" Quint winced when he realized what he'd said.

"You're right, a lion's den would be home for me, whereas a wolf's...not so much. It's good to see you, Mrs. Wilder." He leaned forward and waited for Gerri's kiss on his cheek. He'd seen her enough times to know that was how she preferred to say hello.

"As you want something from me, lion, why not call me Gerri," she said and kissed his cheek. "Hello, Alyx," She turned to the king. "Thank you for inviting me to the party."

Alyx enveloped Gerri in a hug. "You're always welcome in my home. I have you to thank for bringing me my mate after all."

Gerri nodded and gave Quint a strange little smile. "Speaking of mates, I assume you want me to help you find yours, Quint?"

Quint looked at her warily, rumor was when she had a twinkle in her eye, she was up to something.

"I would like that. Do you need to know what I'm looking for in a mate?" He glanced at Alyx, ready to answer whatever questions she had. He wasn't sure how the matchmaking business worked, and he had never thought to ask before.

"Oh yeah, I have a ten-page questionnaire for you to fill out," Gerri replied with a straight face.

"Good god!" Quint looked at Alyx and back to Gerri. Alyx started laughing hard.

"Alyx," Gerri chastised, a wide grin on her face, "You're ruining my fun. Quint, I know exactly what you need. If I decide to find you a mate, you just have to be ready."

Quint nodded, "I guess there's nothing to do but trust your judgment."

She smiled wider. "That is the right way to look at it."

"Even if it goes against my better judgment," he murmured, marching to the Sidaii wine on the table. Yeah, he needed a drink right about now.

"Be prepared to eat those words, pussycat," Gerri said behind him. He turned in time to watch her head to the door. "See you both later."

Once she was gone, he turned to Alyx. "Why do I have a feeling I may both regret and be forever in her debt very soon?"

THREE

Disappointment rushed through her like an arrow to her chest. It was now a fact that Bella was crazy and so was Gerri Wilder. She'd humor the old woman, but damn she'd really hoped she'd get to see a new planet full of sexy shifters.

Gerri actually brought her to the power plant in town. Were they even allowed to be on the premises, wasn't that trespassing or something? Zaria couldn't help but gawk at her surroundings, "Gerri, where are you taking me?"

"Come along, dear, we're almost there." Gerri walked up to the building and knocked on a door. After a moment it opened and Gerri smiled. "Hello, Stephen, thank you for meeting us. Are we all set?"

Stephen had no uniform, but he did wear a suit, so he must be a manager or something. He stepped back and allowed them to enter the building.

"Yes, ma'am, the elevator is waiting on you and everyone else is occupied elsewhere. Have a safe trip."

Zaria just followed along, it was easier at this point. She had to see where this ended, surely the portal wasn't actually in a power plant. Who was she kidding, she didn't think the portal was real at all. They got onto the elevator and Gerri did something at the panel, and they were off. "Gerri, what floor are we going to?"

Zaria glanced at the elevator display, but it didn't show a light lit up or which direction they were heading. "Oh, about 1000 feet down, so your ears might pop a little bit. It's normal and nothing to worry about."

The elevator dinged. Zaria stepped out, her frown unstoppable. "We dropped 1000 feet in seconds? How the hell is that possible?"

Gerri walked down the hall and stopped in front a door that read G. Wilder. "Of course, you would have your own door in a power plant because that is completely normal." What the hell was going on? A power plant? This was insane.

Maybe. Or maybe you're going to another planet full of shifters and visiting Bella. "Maybe I dreamed this whole thing up and I am at home in my bed."

Zaria kept rambling until she saw Gerri pull a small metal egg-shaped thing out of her pocket. She put it up to her mouth and then it flew into the middle of the room, spun fast and a portal formed. Well, at least what she assumed was a portal. It was blue and glowy and wasn't there ten seconds before.

"Close your mouth, dear. Take my hand and we will be in Aurora in just a moment." Zaria reached out automatically and clasped her hand. Ten steps and they were in the blue swirl and then they were in Aurora. Zaria dropped to her knees and heaved a little bit.

"Traveling by portal can be a bit taxing on a human the first time. Take a few deep breaths and relax. It will pass quickly."

Zaria opened her eyes and saw purple trees all around her. All different shades of purple. She stood up and glanced around her. "Holy crap. I'm really not on Earth anymore, am I? This is crazy."

She followed along as Gerri started walking through some trees until she saw it. A palace. What-the-what? Gerri continued toward the palace and Zaria froze in place for a moment. She wasn't kidding. The matchmaker wasn't crazy and neither was Bella. Who knew you could get to another planet through a power plant? Alyx must really be a king and that made Bella the queen. Holy crap on a cracker that was amazing.

"Are you ready to see Bella? I'm sure she's anxious to see you after all this time."

"Uh..."

Gerri eyed her with concern. "Would you like to see your room first and freshen up or Bella? There are guest suites always available and a dress will be provided for you to wear to the party tonight."

"Please take me to Bella, there is so much to take in, I need one familiar sight." Zaria couldn't stop staring as they walked. Good god, this planet had two suns! The colors were more vibrant than anything she had ever seen, not to mention the castle. She craned her neck trying to look at everything.

Everything was so beautiful and a strange combination of antique castle with some amazing modern twists. Some of the stuff along the way she'd never seen in her life. She gaped at everything. The walls, the paintings and tried to soak everything in with each room they passed. Zaria almost bumped into Gerri, she hadn't realized she stopped walking.

"This is the nursery where you will find Bella and the babies. I have to talk to Alyx, I will see you in a few hours." Gerri walked away and Zaria found herself staring at the door. *Should I knock? Just walk in? Are there guards who will attack if I just walk into the room with no warning?* Zaria's mind was whirling with possibilities, she finally decided to do a quick knock and open the door.

Knock.

Knock.

"Bella, are you there? It's me, Zaria." Zaria figured calling out would save her from being jumped by an overzealous guard. "I'm coming in to see you and the babies, please tell me it's safe." She took a few steps in the room and shut the door behind her.

"Zaria!" A scream sounded from somewhere in the massive room. "You're a sight for sore eyes, I can't believe you're finally here." Bella rushed up to Zaria and gave her a hug.

"Bella!" She gasped, hugging her friend tight. "Oh my god," she pulled back and stared at Bella. "You look amazing."

Bella grinned. "Thank you. Married life agrees with me. You look amazing, too. I can't believe it's been so long. I've missed you so much. I did get all your letters, but I couldn't really reply. We're working on a better communication system between us here and Earth family and friends. I hate being unable to communicate with people." Bella hugged her again. "I can't wait for you to meet Alyx and the kids."

Zaria felt tears sting her eyes. "I can't believe you moved to another planet, married a shifter king, and have three babies!"

Bella laughed and pulled Zaria over to the couch. "Sit with me and I will answer any questions you have."

"You better answer my questions! I can't believe I'm here. I went through a portal!" Zaria took a deep breath. "First, where are these babies? Babies! Bella, you have three babies! I'm still in shock. I'm dying to meet them!"

"Avery is the oldest and therefore the future Queen of Aurora, then came Aahron and Aden. You can tell them apart if you look carefully." Bella leaned in and whispered, "Aden has a small birthmark on his right ear, we don't like to make a big deal of it so we don't mention it often. But it helps the family members that don't see them often tell them apart easily."

Bella leaned back and called out to the kids, after a moment they emerged from a corner. The giant room was really several rooms and the children had been playing in the adjacent room. A young woman peeked from around the corner, a wide smile on her face.

"We're good here, Ginnie."

"Yes, ma'am. I'll be over here organizing

some of their toys. Call me if you need."

Zaria gasped at the three cute toddlers and immediately fell in love. "Bella, they are gorgeous and can I hold them? One or all?"

"If one of them holds still long enough for you to grab, go for it," Bella laughed.

She realized then why she said that. The toddlers were a lot faster than human children. They zipped around the room at adult speed. Then one of the boys stopped in front of her and smiled.

She brushed a hand over his beautiful dark hair and he did the sweetest thing. He raised his arms for her to pick up.

"Now there's something you don't see every day," Bella whispered. "Aden wants you to hold him."

She lifted the warm little boy onto her lap and smiled at his beautiful innocent face. "Hi, Aden. I'm Zaria."

"Ria," Aden said in his little baby voice. He grabbed a strand of her hair and brushed it over his cheek. "Soft."

She couldn't help her heart melting and gave him a kiss on top of his head. He wiggled off her lap and went back to playing with his brother and sister.

"Can I just take them home with me, please? It's almost Christmas time, I will spoil them rotten and show them all our traditions." She watched them play and turned to Bella.

God, her biological clock decided at that moment to make itself known. Zaria didn't realize how much she missed Christmas with kids around. Her family were all older and none had little kids so the magic that she loved so much has been missing.

Bella shook her head with a sigh. "There is always someone asking to take my kids, I will tell you what I tell them. Go make your own babies and leave mine."

Zaria giggled at Bella's pout. "Just one problem there, you need a man to make babies and I don't have one."

Bella raised her brows. "Remind me who brought you here today?"

"Very funny. I already teased Gerri about finding me a shifter. I told her I was kidding, though, I am not sure I am ready for that kind of commitment." She would love to find her forever but it was a scary thought, too. There were so many unknowns for her, especially about shifters. Gerri setting her up was a scary but thrilling prospect. "So, are the kids all shifters, too? Hell, are you a shifter now and what kind?"

"We are sure they will be lion shifters, too, but we won't know until they're older for sure. As for me...a girl has to have some secrets," Bella winked. "Let me show you to your room and we can have a glass of Sidaii wine. Trust me, it's delicious and you can relax a bit before the party tonight." Bella pulled Zaria up and linked their arms. "Does that mean there are no men at home waiting for you to return?"

"Men?" She choked. "Men?" Zaria laughed until tears fell down face. "Are you serious? Maybe you have been gone too long to remember the men back home aren't fond of curvy women. At least the ones I have dated, they seem to think I am desperate and will put up with anything they dish out." Wine sounded perfect now, Christmas time was the second worst time of the year to be single. Valentine's Day, of course, being the first.

"You need a shifter. There will be quite a few single men here tonight. Keep an open mind, you never know when you will find the one. Shifters mate for life and you are their whole world. Nothing makes a woman feel more special." Bella sighed and Zaria could tell that she was a woman madly in love with her husband. "The wine is waiting, let's have a drink and get ready for the party together."

"Wine sounds amazing," she sighed, still watching the babies.

"Ginnie," Bella called out. "They're all yours for a bit."

Ginnie nodded and smiled. "No worries, ma'am. I'll start getting them ready for their party soon."

"You're a life saver, Ginnie."

Ginnie flushed and turned to the children, her smile wide.

"She clearly loves your kids," Zaria said as they walked out.

"She does. She's such great help. I can't thank her enough for her support."

FOUR

Quint stood beside Alyx at the triplets' birthday party, watching everyone come in and pay their respects and drop off gifts. The kids didn't seem to be paying attention to the adults. They were torn between eyeing the cupcake table, something Bella adopted from Earth, and trying to grab stuff out of the gifts room. "How long before Aahron tries to grab a present and open it?"

Alyx eyed his children and smirked at Quint. "My money's on Avery, she's as smart as her mom and will convince one of the boys to grab one for her."

"Alyx, are you calling your mate manipulative?" a soft voice said from behind them.

Alyx and Quint turned around to see Bella smiling at them. Alyx pulled Bella into his arms, "Of course not, my love, I was just saying she knows she has the world wrapped around her little finger, much like you."

"Nice save, cousin," Quint whispered. The door opened again and he was hit with the most delicious scent. "Who is that, Alyx? I know she's my mate, but I need a name."

Next to him he could hear them whispering

Bella sighed. "That is a good friend of mine from college, she came to visit me. Be warned, she says she isn't ready for a commitment and is wary of dating a shifter."

Quint didn't bother responding but moved to intercept his mate as she came farther in the room. She was laughing at something to her right and never saw him in front of her. "Oh! Excuse me, I didn't mean to bump into you." Quint closed his eyes, even her voice turned him on.

Mate!

Mate!

Mate!

His lion roared the word repeatedly. It was the craziest fight of his life to not take her then and there.

"What's your name?" Quint growled the words at her, and she recoiled.

"There's no reason to be rude," she snapped. "I already apologized to you." Zaria frowned at him and his lion grumbled his displeasure.

"Tell me your name." Quint tried to backtrack, but it was taking all his strength to hold his lion in check. He wanted to claim his mate now and screw getting her to know him or accept him as her mate.

Zaria stepped back and he followed. "Zaria, I see you have met Alyx's cousin, Quint, and this is my mate, Alyx."

Zaria glanced at Bella, "Quint. Is that who this man is?" She threw him an annoyed look as she pursed her lips. "He didn't give me his name, just demanded to know mine." Zaria turned her body away from Quint and faced Alyx. "It's a pleasure to meet you."

Quint watched as she reached out and shook Alyx's hand. His lion growled again. He didn't like anyone touching his mate, and that included family.

Alyx and Bella laughed at him. They knew he was on edge and they laughed. "Yes. Quint is my cousin. I apologize for his rudeness to you. I guarantee he is not trying to come across as rude."

Quint needed to get her attention back on him. He couldn't believe it. He craved her gaze on him. He needed to see her features change as she spoke and her emotions displayed on her face. "Zaria," he said softly, trying to control his animal, "it's a pleasure to meet you. Please excuse my earlier behavior."

She considered him for a second before giving in. It was as if she had decided to forgive him. Thank fuck! She smiled at him and he reached out to shake her hand.

"It's my pleasure." She took his hand in hers and he groaned quietly at the feel of her soft skin.

Zaria turned to Alyx with a pout. "Alyx, I asked Bella to let me take the triplets home with me. I could show them all our Christmas traditions, it would be so much fun. She said no, though."

Bella poked Alyx in the side. "See, Alyx, there's always someone who wants to take our kids away, I keep telling them to get their own."

Quint caught Bella's glance his way when she said this, but he quickly got back to staring at Zaria. His mate. The thought of anyone else giving her babies was making his lion go nuts.

"I'm not in a rush to have babies, I just want to spoil yours and show them the meaning of Christmas. It's my favorite holiday."

This got Quint's attention, "What's to show them? Humans have made it into a commercialized holiday. It's all about who can buy the biggest and most expensive items. You are kind to each other one day a year and demean, kill and resent each other the rest of the year. I don't get your ideology over this holiday."

Quint was fascinated by the shades of red Zaria's face had turned into while he was speaking.

"Wow, tell me how you really feel. How do you know how we do it on Earth?" Zaria's anger made her eyes sparkle and Quint had a hard time focusing on what she asked him.

Quint couldn't keep his distance, he needed to be closer and using her anger was the perfect excuse. He stepped closer to her, almost touching now. "We have all traveled to Earth a few times, we have studied your traditions. We even have family who live there now, we know all about your commercialized holidays."

"You're not helping yourself," Bella told him with a frown. She wrapped her arms around Zaria and drew her away "Come on. When it comes to Christmas, Quint's a bit of a scrooge. Let's go have a glass of wine. I'm still giddy you're really here. It's almost time for the kids to open the presents anyway."

Quint watched her walk away and he

couldn't stop staring at her. "She is amazing, Alyx, everything I could want in a mate."

"Well, cousin, you riled her up. Good luck getting her to forgive your rant about her favorite holiday. Bella was telling me earlier how important it is to her and you rained on her parade."

Quint grimaced as Alyx laughed at him.

Quint watched Zaria from across the room, every few minutes she would glance at him. She must feel the attraction between them. He wanted her. Needed her. His mate. She'd be his. Only his. He waited till she was alone and walked over to be close to her again.

"Are you enjoying your time in Aurora?"

Zaria glanced up at him, this time she only scrunched her nose at him. "It's beautiful, I haven't seen colors like this before. Do you live here at the palace?"

"The party's winding down, would you be willing to go for a walk with me? I would like to show you my world." She had no reason to say yes, but he hoped the mate pull was strong enough that she felt it, too.

Zaria bit her lip and Quint groaned. He couldn't drag his eyes away from her lips. He'd kill for a taste of her. His animal pushed at his skin. His lion wanted out. Too fucking bad. The man needed to get her attention. He wanted to take that dress off and lick his way up her body, stopping at every curve and savoring every moan.

Her beautiful eyes sparkled with interest. "Sure, I would like to know more about this world Bella now lives in. This is already hard to believe. Seeing more would be fabulous. I'll tell Bella I will see her in a little bit. Okay?"

Quint watched her walk over to Bella and Alyx, then he followed behind. He couldn't stand being far from her, the more he talked to her, the more he craved her.

"I see you've met Zaria. I trust she's in good hands with you." He recognized Gerri's voice behind him.

"Of course. You know she's my mate and nothing comes between that bond. I guess I should thank you now for bringing her here."

"Something tells me this will not be an easy path for you." She patted his arm and gave him a serious look. "Don't fuck up, Quint. I mean it. I keep telling all you men but you all somehow fuck shit up. Just to be clear, I already know you're going to piss her off somehow, so be ready to grovel and win your mate, lion."

Gerri smirked and walked over to Zaria.

"Zaria, I'm in the room next to you, if you need anything just knock on my door. I'm going to talk to the kids for a bit." Quint stared at Zaria who watched Gerri walk away. She shook her head and turned back to Bella.

"That is one strange woman, if you hadn't told me to trust her...anyways, Quint offered to show me around a bit and tell me about Aurora. If it's all right with you that is. I know I came to be here with you, but I am so curious about this planet."

Bella wrapped her arms around Alyx, "Go, love, we can catch up later." Bella caught his eye and winked. She was giving Quint time to get to know his mate.

Quint held his hand out to Zaria and she tentatively reached out for his. His lion instantly relaxed, his mate was close and he was content. For now.

FIVE

Zaria wanted to walk away from Quint, she wanted to avoid him with his shitty attitude about Christmas. But the pull to be close to him was something new and she wanted to see what happened. Was this a shifter thing, could they lure women in with some kind of pheromone? She should have asked Gerri or even Bella.

"It's dark outside but we can tour the grounds a bit and I can tell you about my world if you're interested." Quint stared at her, waiting for a reply she assumed.

She was having trouble paying attention to his words, his eyes drew her in and she was practically panting. He was walking sex and she really wanted a taste, she dropped her eyes to his lips and bit hers.

Would it be wrong to kiss a man she wasn't sure she even liked? Probably. So the very dirty images of him naked were most definitely a big ass no-no. Zaria dragged her eyes back up to his. "That sounds great. Thank you."

Was that really her voice? What did this man do to her? She could be a phone sex operator. Quint must have thought something similar, because she watched his eyes change to a golden color and she felt lust coil in her belly.

Zaria glanced over her shoulder as they walked out of the room and saw Gerri watching them with a slight smirk on her face. *Well, shit. I guess she set me up after all.* This realization made her think twice about Quint. If he was for her, that explained the attraction she felt. *Does this mean I can drag him to my room, jump him and not feel guilty in the morning?*

"Zaria, look up." For a moment she was confused, why would he want her to look up at the ceiling? Then she saw, they were behind the palace and it was dark enough for stars to shine. So many stars. "They are so bright here, is it because it's darker here?"

Quint had moved behind her and she could feel the heat radiating off his body. Against her ear he whispered, "The stars are brighter here, the darkness helps but it could be lit up and you would still see them this clearly." Zaria shuddered and leaned back against him. She let out a slight moan and felt him tense up behind her.

She leaned forward again, she didn't want to come across as pushy, it was just natural to lean against him. Quint's arm went around her waist and pulled her back against his chest. Oh, boy. A hot shudder raced down her spine. This time she felt how attracted he was to her.

"Is that a present in your pants for me?" Zaria couldn't believe the words that just came out of her mouth. She'd never voiced herself that way before. Holy crap, what was happening to her? It had to be the air in Aurora. Or Quint. It was something because she wasn't this bold. Ever. This man was throwing her normal inhibitions out the window. She pushed back against him and felt his cock against her ass. She moaned again.

She needed to distract herself and quickly. Zaria wanted to turn around and release his cock from his pants and drop to her knees, but anyone could see them, right? Yes. She had to keep that thought or she'd do something stupid like climb him like a tree right outside the kid's party. "Tell me how you celebrate Christmas here."

"We don't celebrate the same holiday, obviously, but our version is all about family. If gifts are given, it's something given with love or made with love. We don't buy everything and compete to see who can give the most expensive present. We spend time with family. We help each other out. The holiday is more about giving time, love, help and kindness. It's about giving intangible things or expressions of love that have nothing to do with name brands and price."

"I'm not sure where you got the impression our Christmas was so bad. But everything you said is how we celebrate Christmas, too. Why do you think so badly of humans?" Zaria turned to face Quint, but didn't move back. Every breath he took caused her breasts to rub against his chest, her nipples pebbled and she fought the urge to rub against him like a damn cat.

"I have been to Earth many times, I've seen your malls and stores as people fight over toys, electronics, and other gifts. The advertisements that rave over the hottest toy of the season, and the kids in line to see Santa. They all ask for material items, humans forget the real reason behind the holiday. Family, friends, love and enjoying each other's company." Quint was staring down at her and his eyes were golden again.

"I think you need an education on Earth's customs. You can't judge everyone by a few bad seeds." She gazed up at Quint and lost her train of thought. He stared at her so intensely and that look made her blood heat in her veins. "I...can't remember what I was going to say."

SIX

Quint fought down the lion inside him like never before. Every second he spent next to Zaria was another second his animal wanted to mate her. To stamp his mark on her and show everyone she was his. Taking advantage of her parted lips, he swooped down and kissed her.

Drinking in her gasp, he dipped his tongue into the sweet cavern of her mouth and explored. He threaded his fingers into the soft, dark curls and held her flush against him. Electric currents shocked every blood vessel to life. His cock stood to attention in his pants. She tasted of honey, wine, and sexy woman. His woman. Only his. Her hands strayed up his chest to curl around his neck. She moaned, a ragged little whimper, adding fuel to the fire consuming him.

Quint stepped away and glanced down at her flushed face. They were both panting. She blinked her passion-clouded eyes at him and hastily stepped back.

"What was that for?" The tremor in her voice warmed him. Clearly, the kiss had affected both of them more than he expected.

"I had to know if you tasted as good as you look."

"Oh." She licked her swollen lips and widened her eyes. "And?"

"You taste better than anything I could've imagined."

Zaria stared at him and he wanted to drag her to her room and continue what they started. "I'll walk you to your room, I don't want you to get lost." Zaria nodded her head but didn't move.

"Stop staring at me before I forget my better judgment and take you right now." He clenched his jaw and fought to control his lion, it wanted more of their mate.

Zaria stepped back and sighed. "Tell me about you, what kind of shifter are you?"

Quint turned to the palace and gestured for Zaria to lead, "I'm a lion, king of the jungle. As is my cousin Alyx."

"I remember Bella mentioned the kids would

be lion shifters. I guess I didn't put that together. Family would be the same type, right?" Zaria scrunched her nose up, and Quint wanted to smooth it out and find out what thoughts went through her gorgeous head. He needed to know everything about his woman, his mate.

"Some will marry other types of shifters, so the offspring will be one or the other. Most prefer to mate a human or a shifter like them. I'm not sure how much you know about shifters but we don't pick our mates. Fate does, it's out of our control, but every shifter wants to meet theirs. The bond is the most important aspect of our lives." Quint hoped he was explaining it right, words couldn't adequately describe what mates were to each other. Only the truly lucky ones found their true mate and got to enjoy that bliss.

"It sounds romantic and wonderful. Have mates ever not wanted to be together?"

"Humans typically have a harder time accepting the idea of mates, shifters grow up knowing about them and always looking. Some do spurn their mates, and they can take another, but they will never be able to have children or be fully satisfied."

"Have you found your mate?" Zaria bit her lip and Quint growled quietly.

"If I said I had, but she wasn't ready, what would you say to that?" Quint wanted to tell her she was his and would be forever, but he didn't want to rush her. He saw how his cousin and friends had to tread lightly with their human mates. He wasn't taking a chance she would run. "Here is your room, should I say goodnight now?"

His lion roared. He didn't want to walk away. He wanted to claim her now and keep her forever. Quint felt much the same way.

"Please come in, I would like to talk to you more. I have some wine from earlier if you would like a glass." Zaria opened her door and walked in, glancing at him over her shoulder.

Quint tried to draw his eyes away from her ass as she walked. He could smell her arousal, and it was driving him nuts.

"I don't want any wine." He stalked toward her and spun her around, catching her against his chest. "I need to kiss you again right now."

He stared at her until she nodded permission.

The kiss started out soft and gentle, until she moaned. He couldn't control his hunger. His tongue dueled with hers. "Mine, you are mine."

Quint felt her shiver as he kissed down her neck. He gave her gentle love bites until he was holding her up. He gently moved her back toward the bed, never taking his mouth from her skin.

SEVEN

The backs of her calves brushed the soft material of the bedding. He lowered the straps on her dress and bra, kissed her chest, and made his way down to her breasts. Waves of heat flowed through her veins like molten lava with each swipe of his tongue on her nipple. The dress skimmed her body on its descent to her feet and landed with a swoosh. The bra, which he'd unsnapped at her back without taking his lips off her chest, came off as well.

He licked and laved the tight points. First, he sucked one into his mouth, twirled his tongue on the sensitive tip, and grazed it with his teeth. Liquid fire dripped from her slit. Her pussy throbbed and grasped at the air. She needed him inside soon, or she would start begging. His big hands molded her flesh in his grip. Pinpricks of lust shot through her body and zeroed in on her crotch.

Zaria traced the contours of his lean body, down his muscular chest and to his trousers. She tugged on the material and opened his pants, his hot cock springing free. The pants slid down his legs. Curling a hand around his thick length, she gripped him tight.

"Jesus." He groaned and thrust into her hand. Their gazes met and held. All pretense of waiting was gone. He hissed out a breath and grabbed her by the shoulders, pushing her gently onto her back on the bed. She lay there in her flesh-toned bikini panties and nothing else. He shrugged off his shirt and bent to remove his shoes. Moments later he joined her on the massive bed.

"Please, Quint. I need you." It was no lie. Her body burned with urgency. She fingered her pussy over the wet material of her lacy panties.

His nostrils flared, his gaze zooming in on her hand while she rubbed her clit. The heat of his body caressed the insides of her thighs as he moved between her legs. Breathing heavily, she watched him yank down her underwear. Cool air kissed her heated core, and she shuddered.

Within a heartbeat his lips were on her, kissing and licking around her pussy. She moaned and gripped his hair in her hands, holding him close to her. Need and arousal blindsided her. Needy whimpers rushed past her lips as tension escalated and gathered into a tight knot inside her

"Oh god." She moaned and rocked her hips closer to his lips. A slow fire raged inside her, growing with each lick. Every swipe on her flesh a new spark point ready to trigger her orgasm. His grip on her thighs tightened to keep her from squeezing his head.

"Quint..." Twirls, licks, and sucks drove her so far past the edge she knew she'd fall at any moment. Her hips bucked, rocking harder and faster on him. She choked on each breath, her climax so close she reached for it. That's when Quint sucked on her clit. Hard. The tension inside her unraveled, and her world exploded into colorful shards of bliss. A tide of pleasure rushed her. She screamed and let herself go.

Still panting and quivering from her release, she stared at Quint as he crawled up her body. He gripped his cock and rubbed it over her pussy entrance.

"Oh my," she moaned.

"You like that?"

She licked her lips, letting out a soft groan. "Yessss."

He chuckled. "Want more?"

She frowned, noticing he wasn't moving to enter her. "Yes!"

He lowered until he held himself, skin to skin, over her. When he rocked his hips, his cock slipped and slid between her pussy lips, over her entrance, but no further.

"I will fuck you until you come so hard you won't know what hit you." His words made her entire body shudder and throb.

What the heck could she say? What did it matter? No man had ever made her feel half of what he had in the hours they'd been together. Hours. Dear god. She was so damn easy and didn't even care how she looked right then and there. She just wanted him. More of him. Now.

He slid into her then. His cock stretched her with a delicious friction that hurtled her to the pleasure's edge all over again.

Each thrust brought her closer to the peak. Over and over he slammed into her. She'd lost all train of thought. His movements increased in pace and demand. With each hard thrust his cock lit scorching embers inside her, pushing her to climax.

She whimpered and dug her nails into his slick shoulders. Her orgasm tore through her with the velocity of a freight train. He groaned into her neck and shuddered as he found his own release.

She laid across Quint's chest and drew circles were her fingertips. "I don't usually jump into bed with someone I just met. "

Quint's chest rumbled as he spoke. "You're my mate. We aren't strangers and you couldn't fight the pull for long anyway."

Zaria laid her head down where it was moments ago. She didn't like the sound of this mate business. He made it sound like she had no choice, and she definitely had a choice in who she was with. Scrooge who didn't even like Christmas was not the top of her list.

Sex with him was great, but a man who couldn't even see something like Christmas the way she did…what bigger things didn't they have in common? She wasn't going to find out.

This wasn't forever. This was for now. He was a big boy and knew the deal. She bet he had sex a lot and didn't create a relationship with every woman, so she was no different. They'd scratched an itch, the fact that he just rocked her world…well, that wasn't the important part.

She drifted off to sleep, with the words bah humbug flitting through her mind.

* * *

Zaria woke the next morning to an empty bed. She wasn't surprised or anything, but she hadn't expected him to be the love them and leave them type. Not with all his mate talk the night before. Then again, most men said whatever would get them some. She knew that. Luckily Bella had explained the shower to her yesterday, so she was ready to leave a short time later. After a quick visit to Bella and the babies, she rushed back to her room, half-hoping Quint had returned. No such luck. Her heart sank a little, but she brushed it off. With still no word from Quint, she knocked on Gerri's door.

"Good morning, Gerri," she called as Gerri opened the door. "Are we leaving early today? I would like to get home to start decorating for Christmas. With luck, I can convince Bella to bring the babies over to see it."

Gerri's musical laugh filled the hallway Zaria stood in. "We can go whenever you want. I told Bella I would bring you back anytime you were ready to visit. Is there anyone you want to say goodbye to before we leave, my dear?"

"No, thank you, though. Bella and I do not say goodbye, because we will always see each other again soon." No way was she hunting down Quint. If he was too good to be in her bed when she woke up, then he was not worth her time. Besides, he was a total scrooge. He'd spurned her love of Christmas and she wouldn't give him another thought. "Do we get home through the portal again, Gerri? Back to the forest I mean?"

"Follow me, dear, this won't take long at all." Zaria had the feeling Gerri was speaking about more than just the portal home with that statement, but she couldn't figure out what. "I just want to drop this letter off with someone to deliver for me. I'm sure we will pass someone on our way out."

EIGHT

"Alyx, where is Zaria? I went by her room and it's empty." Quint ran his hands through his hair, making it stand on end. "I need to talk to her." Quint paced the room and glared at Alyx.

"She went home with Gerri already. Bella said she had things to do for Christmas and there was no reason for her to stick around here." Alyx raised an eyebrow at Quint. "What did you do?"

"Besides criticizing her favorite holiday? I had to take care of a small dispute between some cubs. Nothing big, just doing my job. I should have left her a note before I left this morning."

Alyx raised both brows before shaking his head slowly. "You left her in bed alone, with no note saying why or telling her you would be back? You have some groveling to do."

Quint growled. "I'm going to Earth. I need to see her. Will Gerri help me find her? Will you have Karel cover my territories for me?"

Alyx grinned. "Go with my blessing and I'm sure after Gerri is done chewing you up, she will help you find your mate."

* * *

A few hours later, he stood outside Gerri's door waiting for her to answer. His lion wouldn't stop growling, he wanted his mate now and he was pissed she left them. Hadn't she understood what he'd told her about mates? What he'd explained? Maybe she didn't want to be his mate. His chest compressed at the idea.

"Took you long enough to get here," Gerri snapped, her eyes blazing. "I told you not to mess up and you managed it in the first day." She shook her head and opened the door wide. "Come inside if you want my help." Quint let out a relieved breath and walked into her apartment, following Gerri to a living area. "Please have a seat and enjoy a sugar cookie, they're fresh. I made them the minute I got here so you could have something to eat when you came to your senses."

Quint didn't want a fucking cookie! Dammit. His lion was pissed. He was pissed. Anxiety weighed his stomach with rocks. Still, he didn't want to anger Gerri any further, so he took one anyway. "Tell me where she lives and I'll go find her."

"Not so fast. Why should I give you a second chance when you blew the first? Rather quickly, I might add. And I'll break it down to your furry ears so you understand. Your ranting over human traditions and how a few celebrate the holiday upset a person who genuinely loves Christmas. She loves the magical way it brings people together. The love and kindness. You ignored the vast majority see it as a family time and about giving not receiving." Gerri smirked for a second. "Giving and receiving presents, I mean."

Quint couldn't deny these accusations, so he just waited for her to finish chewing on his hide.

"Then you give her what she said was the best orgasm of her life and possibly ruined her for all other males. Stop grinning before I turn you into a Sphynx. You commit a crime by leaving her to wake up alone." Gerri's glare could melt the top of the mountains.

"Shit," he dropped his gaze to the cookie at hand. "I thought I'd be back this morning before she woke up. I didn't think she would leave so fast either. I wanted to talk to her, apologize for my words and tell her she was my mate." His lion roared and Quint winced. "She better not even think about another man giving her an orgasm. They belong to me and me alone."

Quint glanced up to see Gerri smiling at him. "Those were the right answers." She handed him a slip of paper. "Her address is listed on that. Prepare to grovel. When I left her, she was swearing to skin you alive. I'm sure Bella gave her that idea, too."

"I need one more favor from you, can you coordinate a few things for me back home? I want to bring her home with me and show her my Christmas. I didn't get a chance to do anything before I left, though."

Gerri's eyes twinkled, "I'm happy to help with this, just tell me what you want and where."

* * *

It took some maneuvering, but after updating his Earth communicator GPS, he was able to move around. He frowned when he found himself standing outside Zaria's apartment. Third floor, fourth door on the right his mate waited for him. Whether she knew it or not. His lion knew she was close and he was barely containing him. He made his way inside and up the stairs, he would move faster than the elevator and he was beyond capable of waiting when she was so close.

He knocked and waited, then waited a few more minutes. Once his patience wore thin, he knocked harder. "Zaria, I know you're there," he told the door. "I can scent you. I need to talk to you."

Someone opened the door a few feet away and an elderly woman in pink hair rollers wearing footie cat pajamas and holding a kitten stared at him. "What did you do?"

"Excuse me?" He didn't have time for small talk with strangers.

"What did you do to Zaria? She's the kindest person I know. So what did you do that she's not opening the door to you?"

"I'd rather not say."

Her frown deepened. "But are you sorry?"

He ground his teeth and gave a sharp nod. The woman's face transformed, and she gave him a wide smile. "Oh, well good. She's a good girl. Be good to her."

And just like that, she was back in her home and he was still waiting for Zaria to open her door. He could definitely smell her and knew she was inside. "Please open the door, I can hear you breathing on the other side."

The door burst open and a furious Zaria glared at him, her chest heaving and her eyes flashing fire. God, she was fucking gorgeous. "You can hear me breathing? That's all kinds of fucked up. What are you doing here anyways?"

He stalked toward her, causing her to back up and he slammed the door shut behind him. He kept stalking her until she hit a wall, the anger he'd scented was gone, but her frown was still there. The bravado in place didn't budge. "Why did you run from me? Did you not think I would come after you, mate?"

Zaria's voice quivered "Mate? Did you call me your mate?"

Quint growled, "You're mine. I told you that. You. Are. Mine."

"But you don't even know me. I don't know you. And half of what I do know," she glared at him again, "I don't particularly like."

"And what half *do* you like?" He licked his lips and watched desire spring to life in her gaze.

"How can we be mates? I mean I know what you said last night, but it's not that easy for me to just say 'sure, I'm yours forever.'" She put her hands on his chest to push him away but he leaned in so she was trapped against his chest, her hands pinned.

"I want you, my lion wants you. There is

nothing else important for me."

The desire in her gaze dimmed, replaced by insecurity. "There is for me, though. I want love and not just fate telling me we belong together. Yes, I am attracted to you, but I need more."

Quint growled and moved off of her, then paced to the other side of the room. "Fine. What do I have to do to prove to you we belong together? That you are mine, and I'm yours forever?"

NINE

When Quint growled those words, Zaria's knees went weak. She wanted to pounce on him and ravage his gorgeous body. She eyed his cock straining against his jeans. *If I want it, that is all for me. If I take it, it's mine. He's mine. But at what price?* She dragged her eyes away and looked him in the eye.

"Court me. Date me. Show me."

Quint looked shocked for a moment. "What the fuck does that actually mean?"

Zaria sighed. "Let's go on a few dates. Get to know each other the way humans do. Not just sniffing each other and claiming them."

Quint stalked toward her again, the sight of

his golden eyes sent lust coursing through her body. "We don't sniff and claim our mates. We lick them...all over. Then when you are screaming from your release, I will bite, stamp you and cum in your warm pussy. Then you will be mine and I will be yours."

Zaria was sure she came from his words alone, the thought of his thick cock inside her again, making her scream was exactly what she wanted. She couldn't keep her distance any longer, she wrapped her arms around his neck and kissed him. He growled and pressed against her body, his cock nestled against her. She sucked in a breath and let out a rough moan.

Their tongues tangled and she lifted her legs to wrap around his waist. It went on that way for what felt like an hour before common sense hit her upside the head and she realized she needed to get a hold of herself.

After a few minutes, she pulled her mouth away and rested her forehead on his chest. "You're a dangerous man, Quint."

"Why?" he whispered.

"You make me forget everything. My mind just empties of everything but you."

Quint laughed and his chest rumbled, rubbing against her breasts. Her nipples pebbled and she groaned at the friction.

"Let me show you how most people really celebrate Christmas. If you still think we don't do the holiday right…I'm not sure I can be with you."

Quint growled, "Nothing as stupid as that will keep me from you. You are mine."

She sucked in an angry breath and lifted her gaze to meet his, frustration riding her blood. "It's not stupid and I didn't say keep you from me. It's my choice to accept you as my mate, right?"

Quint gave a sharp nod, his features like carved stone.

"I can't be with someone who mocks my values and traditions. It means you don't care about what I want, or love. That shows me you would be dismissive of other areas of our life together. Does that make sense?"

"I would never do that intentionally," he scowled. "I don't agree with you but I understand where you are coming from. If this is what you need, then I will do it."

The anxiety in the pit of her stomach lessened at his words. "Thank you, Quint. Mates may mean instant attraction and desire to be near each other, but it doesn't say love. I *need* that. Sex will not give that to me. No matter how great it is. I need to know you. And you need to know me if this is going to work between us."

Determination filled his gaze. "Be ready at seven pm for our first date. Keep an open mind. I will do the same." Zaria watched Quint march out her door. She was confused, excited, scared and horny. So many emotions caused by one man.

She glanced at the clock. It was only three pm. She had four hours until her first date with Quint. Not sex, though that sounded freaking amazing, too, but a real fucking date. Her head spun from thinking about it. She had enough time for some pampering and waxing. Just because they had scorching sex didn't mean she couldn't pull out all the stops.

She grabbed her jacket and headed to her favorite salon, hopefully, they could fit her in fast.

The salon was only a block away so she decided to walk over and use the fresh air to clear her head of Sexy Quint thoughts and the recurring visuals of their night of hot sex.

The fresh air didn't seem to work. She was at the salon door before she knew it and she didn't recall the walk at all. She pulled open the door and smiled when the bell jingled. It always made her think of Santa's sleigh bells.

"Hello, Zaria, my darling! It's been too long, what brings you by today?" Zaria couldn't help the smile that bloomed across face. Reggie was her favorite stylist, and usually booked up weeks in advance. Just her luck he was free today.

"Reggie, I'm so excited to see you. I have a date tonight and I need the works."

"Whoa, hunny! The works, this must be some date. Is it serious?" Reggie's over-the-top theatrics always relaxed Zaria and made her smile.

She bit her lip but couldn't help grinning again. "Yes, I think it's very serious, or could easily be. He may be the one if he plays his cards right."

Reggie ushered her to his station, "If he has a brother who is my type give him my number, love. Fuck it, just tie him up and FedEx him to my house. I'll handle the rest."

She giggled as did several other women. "You're too much, Reggie."

He winked. "Girl, if I can get me a man like the one that's got you glowing like that, I'm gonna keep him. Whether he wants me to or not. Now let's get started."

TEN

Quint paced in front of Zaria's apartment. Who knew courting a woman could make a man crazy nervous? The lion roared deep inside him. Damn nerves. He would win his woman on her terms, whatever it took to claim her. His lion was agitated, too, he wanted to claim her now. Fuck waiting. He stopped in front of her door and knocked.

When the door opened, his breath was knocked out of his chest. "You're glowing, you're always beautiful but you glow now."

Zaria blushed, making her even more breathtaking to look at. "Would you like to come in or are you ready to go?"

"Let's go before I kiss the lipstick off your

luscious lips, drag you to the closest flat surface and fuck you senseless." The scent of Zaria's arousal made his lion roar. And damn if he didn't want to roar, too.

Zaria stepped outside, pulling the door shut behind her, but he hadn't moved back so she was flush against his chest and the door. "Tonight, we continue where we

left off earlier, unless you tell me otherwise. I want to lick you until you're panting," he whispered against her lips. "And then I'll slip my cock into your wet heat and bend you over the couch. Fuck your slick pussy until you scream my name."

Zaria's breath panted out and he skimmed his lips over her jaw and up to her ear, "And you will." He nipped at her earlobe. "You will scream my name."

The words repeated themselves inside her head like a broken record. Then he stepped back and gave her room to lock her door. Her hands shook, so it took a minute.

"I want to celebrate everything that makes your Christmas so special to you. Bella was willing to help, so I hope you are pleased. Tonight, we are going to a Christmas tree lighting ceremony in a park. They have vendors and crafts set up, too. I thought we could walk around and enjoy the sights together."

Quint realized he probably sounded like a pup wet around the ears, but his mate was the most important thing and he would use any tool to gain her love and acceptance. Bella was easy to convince, though, she offered up ideas and typical things Zaria did to celebrate. They left her building and started walking toward the street.

"Quint, how long are you staying here? Do you have to go back to Aurora soon?" Zaria was biting her lip again. Quint didn't even bother not staring. As they walked, he realized she didn't know how sexy she was. Everything about her was natural and unpretentious. She might not realize how beautiful her openness made her, but the men around them did. He swallowed a growl, not happy they stared at his mate.

"Let's take a taxi and I will tell you more about me. Okay?" He really wanted to get her out of viewing range of the men walking outside her apartment building.

To his shock, Zaria turned and whistled for a cab. Within seconds one was idling at the curb. She turned with a saucy wink and climbed in. There was a lot more to his mate than he realized.

Quint got in next to her and turned to angle his body toward her. "I will stay as long as it takes to convince you to come to Aurora with me. See my home, what it's like, and maybe you will fall in love with it and me."

She worried her lip, her gloved hands folded on her lap. "I know Bella was able to move, but she wasn't as attached to Earth as I am. I don't know if I can give up my life here, away from my family and everything I have known."

"Just give it time, please. We will take it one day at a time." He turned to the driver. "Green Acres Park, please." Quint sat back and wrapped his arm around Zaria, pulling her close.

"What do you do in Aurora?" Zaria was looking up into his face and he couldn't resist dropping a kiss on her lips. When she groaned, he took that as a sign to deepen the kiss and slid his tongue between her lips. They kissed for a while. When the car stopped, he didn't. At least, not until the taxi driver cleared his throat and they broke apart.

"Quint, did you bring human money with you to pay?" Zaria whispered. He assumed she didn't want the driver to hear her words.

He smirked at her and handed a folded bill to the driver, "Keep the change and Merry Christmas."

Zaria climbed out behind him. "In Aurora I would be what you call police or a sheriff. I move around Alyx's territory and handle any disputes."

"Wouldn't that be Alyx's job as king?" Quint

hoped her question meant she was wanting to learn about his world because she would soon be a part of it.

"Alyx handles all the big problems or anything that would require mediation. Karel is his head of security at the castle and between species. I'm only for the lion pride. I just handle things on a smaller scale. Nothing that will threaten the planet. I take care of issues and move them up the ladder along with requests and the like to Alyx as needed. For his safety, we don't like him just traveling around without guards. When he does go out, everyone wants to talk to him. That means he doesn't always get to hear the people's problems."

Zaria frowned. "I guess that makes sense. I never really thought about that before."

Quint put his arm around her shoulders and walked toward the giant Christmas tree in the center of the park. "It's almost time for the tree to be lit."

They stood in front of the tree, watching the little kids bundled up in colorful coats, gloves and scarves run around and scream. Each time Zaria's face lit up.

"Aren't they adorable?" She laughed watching the kids fall over themselves in the snow.

"You want kids when we mate? I can give you as many as you want but at least four. Making babies could take a lot of time and I'm happy to do that." The scent of Zaria's arousal never really faded but at his words, it got stronger and he growled.

"I think you have an admirer, Quint." He dragged his eyes away from her and glanced down. In front of him stood a little girl, he guessed around three or so. Quint squatted down in front of her, "Hi."

"Hi, mister, you growled. Are you an animal?" The little girl had a huge smile on her face, he wondered if she was aware of shifters.

"Do you think I am?" Zaria laughed above him and he tilted his head up to smirk at her.

"My name is Jolie," she said, her little voice full of interest. "Are you a tiger?"

Quint laughed at that. "Have you ever met a tiger, little one?"

"My mom is dating a shifter. He's big like you. She told me he is an animal and a human." That made sense to him, at least explained how she knew about animals and humans.

"No, little one, I am a lion."

She gave him an even bigger smile. "A big kitty. Okay."

Zaria giggled as the little girl took off to play with the other kids in the snow.

Quint stood up and watched her for a minute.

"You were wonderful with her, big kitty."

"I'll show you kitty," he growled and dipped her. At her squeal, he took the opportunity to kiss her open lips like a famous black and white Earth photo he'd seen of a sailor and a nurse after World War II. There were a couple of 'awws' and a few claps while he kissed her.

They straightened and he wrapped his arm around Zaria and leaned close. "Imagine how good I would be with our cubs. The ones I am going to enjoy making with you as often as we can." He felt her shudder slightly and his lion roared in approval.

"Naughty kitty," she whimpered. "You fight dirty."

Yes. Yes, he did. Quint smiled and turned back to the tree and the kids playing.

ELEVEN

Zaria looked around at the families and couples staring at each other and the tree. Her heart squeezed and her insides warmed. This was what she'd always wanted. Someone to hold her hand while doing Christmas stuff. Someone to drive away the loneliness. And here he was. But for how long?

Her family didn't enjoy the holidays like they used to, everyone did their own thing. This year her parents were going to Florida to sit on the beach. She didn't begrudge them that. They'd worked hard to be able to do that.

Still, she missed family gatherings and everyone laughing and doing things together around the tree. She missed making cookies for her cousins. She missed wrapping gifts for her little nieces and nephews. With them now in college, things changed.

Now, they were big and going on skiing trips with their boyfriend and girlfriends. Aunt Zaria wasn't as important as she used to be when they were kids. She needed her own children to show the values of family and giving. But was Quint the right man to create that foundation with?

Zaria listened with half an ear as the host of the Christmas tree lighting ceremony talked, her gaze wandered to Quint and she couldn't look away. She could have everything she wanted with him, if she was willing to give up her life on Earth, her family, friends. She worried moving away to another planet would cause her to lose herself, her own identity. Was he worth that risk?

Quint glanced at her, his gorgeous eyes glowing. "They're pushing the button now, look."

She turned back to the tree just as it lit up. "It's so beautiful."

It brought a wide smile to her face. One of the things she loved most was that this time of the year everyone was just a bit nicer to each other.

"No, love. You're beautiful. Are you ready to walk around and look at the vendors?" Quint took her hand and started walking, a young couple looked over and smiled at them.

"Quint, tell me about your home on Aurora. Do you live in the palace, or do you have your own place?"

"I live in a cottage."

She frowned. "A cottage? Like a mobile home?"

"No. It's a house, but it's not huge. I've never needed more than the space there. It's perfect. You'd love it. We can easily add to make it larger as we have kids. A nursery. A playroom. Whatever you want. We can make it your dream. Just outside my front door is a small lake that ices over in the winter. The palace isn't far so I can easily walk over and talk with Alyx when I need to."

Quint smiled when he talked about home, to Zaria it showed his love for it.

"It sounds wonderful, so different than here for sure. Living in the city can be tiring, always around people, the smog, the crowds. Sometimes, I want to get away but still be close to civilization." Zaria stopped in front of a vendor selling handmade customized ornaments.

"Do you put up Christmas trees at home? I was thinking of getting an ornament for Bella with the kids' names on it."

Quint looked at the table, "What about this

one, it has room for Alyx, Bella and the triplets."

"Yes! That would be perfect. Thank you, Quint." Before she could grab her wallet, Quint paid for it and presented it to her.

She shook her head but took it with a smile. "You didn't have to pay, I was happy to. They're my friends."

Quint leaned down and whispered in her ear. "I will always take care of you, my mate. Anything you want is yours."

Zaria turned to look at him. He was offering her everything she'd ever wanted. It was messing with her head and her emotions. Logic dictated she take it nice and slow and think it through. Emotions told her to grab on and take him home. Emotions won. "Take me home and make me yours for tonight."

Quint growled and tugged her back through the park, his growl made her wet and she was ready to jump his bones. He pulled her into a darkened spot and stopped behind a massive tree, tugging her close.

"I can smell your arousal and I need to taste you. Now."

They kissed and he groaned, making her instantly hot.

She wrapped her hands around his neck and clung tight to him. He pushed her back against a large tree. Her body rubbed against his in mind-blowing caresses, she couldn't stop the moan. He slid his hands under her coat, up from her waist, to cup her breasts.

Fuck, she'd been dying for him touch her all night. She'd expected his fingers to be cold from the weather, but he was nice and warm. The heat emanating from his body made her want to strip on the spot. Her coat was suddenly wide open. The cold didn't penetrate their warm bubble.

She wore a top that allowed her breasts to play peekaboo and she'd been waiting for him to see it. Her original idea was to drive him crazy with need, but with the cold weather it had been hard. Until now. It had definitely been worth the wait. He grabbed a handful of her breasts and squeezed.

Jesus-fucking-hell, she was burning up. His cock was steel hard, she could feel it at the junction of her thighs. Rational thought fled her brain. She didn't care they were in a public park, or that anyone could see them. It actually made her hotter. Good god! She'd no idea it would excite her for someone to watch them.

Quint must have realized where they were at the same time and pulled back from their kiss. "Let's go, we need to get back to your place now or I'll take you standing right here."

Zaria was focused on the feeling of his hand

in hers. She didn't pay attention to the walk back toward the crowd of park goers. Or the ornaments she'd been fascinated with before. She definitely didn't pay attention to a cab arriving, driving them home or walking into her apartment building.

This man scrambled her senses and all she could think about was having him close, touching her, riding his cock until she screamed in pleasure.

"Zaria, give me your key or open the door. I need to be inside you now, I can't wait any longer to feel your body against mine." Zaria pulled the keys out of her purse and handed them to Quint, her hands shaking worse than before. It would be twice as hard to get the door open and the last thing she wanted was to waste time.

With a growl he shoved the key in, pushed the door open and dragged her inside. She kicked the door shut behind them and leaned back against it. Quint moved so he was flush against her body again, "Are you sure you want this right now?"

Zaria didn't reply, just leaned up and kissed him. The kiss — dear God, what a kiss — was better than any of the previous ones. This was full of hunger. Passion. Need. An expectation of wants being met that made her pussy slick. It was as if the animal side of him had taken control.

She loved it. The speed with which her coat and gloves came off. His next. The way he slid his hand down her arms to the edge of her top. The warmth of his hands when he pulled the material up and above her head.

Their kiss broke for all of a second before their lips were once again pressed together, tongues rubbing and breaths mingling. She gripped his shirt in her hands, the material soft yet annoying. There was too much between her hands and his body. She wanted it all out of the way.

She tugged on his shirt, until he got the hint and the thing came off. A sigh fell from her lips at the feel of his warm smooth skin. Blazing need pooled at her core. Her body vibrated with desire for Quint. This thirst for his touch, it was unlike anything she'd ever experienced before. Somehow, someway, he'd managed to reach deeper in a few days than other men had in the span of months.

Bone-deep desire for the man sliding his hands up her back and removing her bra grew with each of her breaths. His abs contracted under her palms. She glided her hands up his chest, through the slight mat of hair and scored her nails down his pecs.

A loud hoarse groan sounded from him. He

broke their kiss, eyes bright with a hunger she loved seeing in their depths. Her bra came off and his gaze slowly trailed down to her tits.

"You are by far the most beautiful woman I've ever seen."

She couldn't say if it was the way he said the words, with so much honesty, but hearing him say it and watching his expression fill with lust broke her control.

"Touch me, please," she begged in a soft cry.

"I can do better than touching," he murmured. "I can lick, suck and fuck you for the rest of my life. Your body is an addiction I never want to give up."

He yanked on the button to her pants, pulling them and her panties down her legs. He didn't give her a chance to enjoy the heated smile over his lips. He led her to a big brown sofa against the wall. The backs of her legs hit the sofa and she fell on the cushion. She tugged on the fly of his jeans. The pants fell down his legs and that's when she realized he went commando. Hot damn!

"My god," she gasped.

Breaths rushed out of her lungs while she tried to take in the entire vision of his body. His very big body with those really mind-muddling muscles. He was way past sexy and into hot damn of body categories. With his slightly hairy chest, legs and arms, he made her fantasize while being wide-awake.

Then there was his cock. Large, stiff and with beads of pre-cum dripping from the slit. Her throat went dry with every peek she took at his shaft. To make things more interesting, she'd swear the more she looked at it, the harder and bigger it got.

"I need you to touch me, Zaria," he whispered. "I want your soft little hands on me. On my cock."

She raised a hand to touch him, stroking the hot hard length of him. She grasped him tight in her hand, moving her hand up and down his shaft. Once she got to the tip, she wet her thumb with the moisture dripping from his slit and rubbed it over the head of his cock.

She moved closer, ready to take him in her mouth, but he grabbed her face in his hands, forcing her to look up at him. He shook his head and dropped down to his knees, moving his hands to her thighs, pushing her legs wide open.

"Not yet, beautiful," he said in a low, gruff whisper. "I need to taste you before I lose my control."

His features tightened with need. He was

losing control over her. Her. Not some other woman. A primitive need to lose her own control along with him pushed her to act. She slid her fingers into his hair, gripping and tugging him up to her.

A new clash of their lips and she was on fire. He cupped her breasts, thumbing her nipples roughly. The ache in her pussy grew by leaps and bounds. She wanted him to fill her with his cock. She needed to be his.

She tugged her face to the side, breaking their kiss and moaning. "Please."

Dear God, if she didn't get him inside her soon she might explode. He slid his lips down her jaw. Biting. Kissing. Licking.

Wetness dripped from her pussy. She was soaked. He sucked a nipple into his mouth and fireworks went off behind her lids. "Yes! Keep doing that. I like your mouth on my tits."

The roughness of his stubble combined with the painful bite from his teeth shot electric currents from her nipples to her clit. Intense arousal shook her to the core.

He squeezed her tits together, licking and sucking from one nipple to the other. The delightful torture only intensified her desperation.

"For the love of sanity, fuck me. Please..."

She sucked in breaths, trying to keep her brain in working order but the reality was she was so far gone nothing could help. Nothing but his body taking hers. Owning hers.

"Quint...I need more," she groaned.

He lifted his head from her breast, her nipple still in his mouth, and let go with a resounding pop.

"Your skin tastes so fucking good. Like hot sex and fresh berries." He kissed the valley of her breasts and ran circles with his tongue down her belly. At the juncture of her thighs, he pushed her legs open and stared at her pussy. He inhaled and groaned.

Quint caressed her inner thigh, heating her to the core with his penetrating stare. "You're beautiful, Zaria. Every single inch of you makes my mouth water. I want you. I want to fuck you in every way possible," he said the words as a promise. "I want to slide so deep in you there will be nothing between us."

"Quint..." she called to him in a soft whimper. "Please..."

His head dropped between her legs. He treated her large thighs with such gentleness, spreading them wider and displaying her for his view. His breath caressed her pussy. He curled his arms around her thighs and she ended up with her legs over his big shoulders.

"How badly do you want me to lick your pussy, darling?" His words taunted her.

"I want it so bad. More than anything," she whimpered. "Suck it, lick it, and bite it. Do it all. I don't care, just do something before I die waiting to come." She groaned, tilting her hips, trying to reach his lips. She needed that touch. His mouth on her twitching clit. Her muscles burned with need.

Right when she thought she couldn't possibly survive another second without his touch, his lips grazed her pussy in a kiss so light she moaned at the torture. "You're so evil..."

He chuckled. The laughter caused his shoulders and her legs to shake with the movement.

"Baby." He kissed the hard nubbin of her desire. "You have no idea how good I can be."

She gripped his short hair in her fists. "I don't want to hear how good you are," she panted. "Show me."

He licked her pussy again. Harder. Rougher. He splayed his tongue flat and swiped it up from ass to clit in a blood boiling lick meant to reduce her brain cells to jelly.

"Oh. My. God!"

There was no stopping her whimpers any longer. Nor the wiggling of her hips as he rolled his tongue over her clit then down to her entrance, sucking at her sleek core, making slurping noises she was even more turned on by.

A loud rumble sounded from his chest as he fucked her pussy with his tongue. She pushed back into the sofa, her muscles almost locking from the quick rise to the edge.

The delicious torture didn't stop there. He slid a finger into her, hooking it and rubbing her insides at the same time he sucked on her clit.

She didn't get a single warning. The winding tension at her core snapped to the point she was shoved into the wild waves of pleasure. She screamed louder than she ever had. A call for Quint tore from her throat.

The orgasm pushed to the forefront, taking her breath away. An explosion of desire washed over her tense muscles, cooling her sizzling pores as her legs shook on his shoulders. It was unlike any other experience. No man had ever made her body's need for him scorch her from the inside. There had never been an orgasm that left her spent. Her body ached as though she'd run miles and worked out like she hadn't in years.

"Christ!"

She blinked her vision back into focus and

watched Quint slide his cheek on her thigh. Then he kissed her and repeated it with her other thigh.

She leaned forward, cupping his face in her hands and kissing him, enjoying the taste of her own body on his lips.

"Mmm."

With a gentle push, she got him to lay back on the carpet, their kiss unbroken. She met his gaze. His eyes had gone the color of the most clear-cut emeralds. Beautiful. It was the way he stared at her that made her breath catch in her chest. Like she was the sexiest woman in the world and he never wanted to look away.

The heat of his gaze and the hardness of his arousal were like pulsing electrical currents through her veins.

TWELVE

She straddled him, stroking her slick pussy over his cock in a slow glide. "Fuck!" he groaned.

He grabbed her tits and fondled her, tweaking her nipples with his calloused thumbs. She curved into his touch, moving her body forward.

"Oh, yes. Do that. I like when you tug on my nipples," she moaned.

He did it again. "Sweetheart, you need to let me in you or I will embarrass myself if you keep sliding yourself on my dick."

She lifted her hips and grabbed his slick cock with one hand to place it at the entrance of her sex. He pulsed in her hand, hard and hot. She met his gaze, a world of communication happened without either saying a word. Then, she pressed down. For every inch she slid down, her lungs burned hotter. She dug her nails into the mat of hair on his chest, using him for leverage.

"Oh, God..."

He slid his hands down from tweaking her nipples to hold her by the waist.

"I'm sorry, darling," he bit out through his clenched jaw.

"Why?" she asked with a gasp. The feeling of being stretched overpowered her senses.

"I can't do slow any longer," he growled. All of a sudden the world shifted. She was on her back with Quint pumping deep into her from above. She gasped as he pressed his cock further and further, until she could swear there wasn't a single inch of space in her he couldn't reach.

He groaned, "Fuck, you feel so good."

Brushing his lips on the side of her neck, he pulled back. The quick thrust that followed tore a moan from her. She gripped his slick arms, digging her nails in an unforgiving bite. He licked her shoulder, grazing his teeth over her hot skin.

"Yes!" she encouraged. "More. Do me harder."

"Fuck, sweetheart. You're so tight I'm

having a hard time controlling myself."

Control? What control? She'd given up on control a long time ago.

He thrust and propelled back.

Deeper.

Harder.

Faster.

It was heaven. It was hell. It was everything she'd ever wanted and never dared hope for.

The sliding of his body over hers turned into a reminder of how delectable it was to have him filling her, taking her. Breaths puffed out of her lips in short quick bursts.

He lowered his head and kissed her, skating his tongue over her lips. In and out of her mouth in tandem with each plunge of his cock into her. Hunger expanded in her chest almost to near bursting. A new craving had taken over her body. She needed to come. Had to have him make her reach that peak she rarely got to go with a man.

Almost as if he'd read her mind, his drives turned harsher, animalistic. A rumble sounded from his chest. His lion was close to the surface and that only made him wilder. Lust raged inside her, blacking out everything but him. His body pressed her to the rug. He skimmed his hands up to her face to hold her head at the angle he wanted for his kisses.

A storm brewed in her blood. Then came that moment where her muscles tightened. She broke their kiss, searching for much needed air.

"Oh, Quint..." she choked.

He nibbled on her jaw and earlobe. "Come. Your body's ready and I want to feel your pussy tight on my cock."

She couldn't breathe or think or do more than feel the tension snap and a flood of pleasure assault her. A loud moan rushed up her throat and left her dry lips. Stars burst in the backs of her lids. The world slowed to a crawl where only the sound of her heartbeats filled her ears.

His thrusts slowed. His body tensed above hers. Their gazes met. An inexplicable connection cemented itself between them. He threw his head back and roared at the same time his cock pulsed inside her. Streams of cum filled her channel with his seed. He rolled them over, still inside her, until she lay on top of him again.

They stayed that way for what felt like hours but was probably more like a few minutes, trying to catch their breaths.

"Sleep, my love, we will talk in the morning."

THIRTEEN

She didn't remember getting into bed last night, but that was where she was, her comfy bed. Thank god, waking up on the floor would have been very uncomfortable. She stretched her body and felt the empty space next to her. *Bastard better not have left me again.* "Quint, where are you?"

No reply after a minute so she got up to search her apartment. The bathroom was empty as was the kitchen. Sitting on the table, though, was a note:

My Love, I had to check in back home. I will be gone a few hours, be ready for our second date at six pm. Dress casually but warm, we are going to have fun.

All my love,
Quint.

She couldn't be upset with him, since he left a note. Zaria wished she could talk to Bella about all this information, shifters, mating. It was a lot to take in. Then it hit her, why not Gerri? She would be able to answer any questions.

One shower and an hour later, Zaria stood outside Gerri's door waiting on her to open the door. She didn't expect for Gerri's voice to come from outside her home.

"Good morning, Zaria. I was expecting you, so I ran to the bakery to get some scones for us to enjoy."

Zaria spun around to see Gerri coming down the hallway. "Good morning, Gerri. I hope it's okay I stopped by. I needed to talk to someone and you were the only one I knew who could help or understand my questions."

"Hold the bag while I unlock the door. I am happy you came to me and will help anyway I can." They walked in the apartment and Gerri gestured to the couch. "Have a seat, I will get us some plates and coffee."

Gerri had already hung a wool coat by the door. Zaria sat down and took her coat off, setting it beside her on the seat. She thought about the first time she sat on this couch. So much had changed, she had really thought Gerri was crazy when she first met her. Now look at her, dating a shifter, thinking about moving to another planet to mate that shifter. She was the crazy one!

"First, I must ask how the lion is treating you. Has he made you roar yet?" Gerri laughed when Zaria blushed.

"I…uh…what?"

Gerri grinned wide. "You heard me, girl. Speak."

She blinked wide eyes at Gerri. "I'm sorry. I'm not used to a woman being so frank, well, at least not older woman."

Gerri waved her words away, "A bunch of prudes! I notice you didn't answer my question. Hmmm."

Shit. No way to avoid it.

"I think the roaring has been mutual, several times." Zaria couldn't believe she was talking with Gerri about her sex life. "I came here to talk to you about mates and love, though."

Gerri raised an eyebrow at Zaria. "Ask me anything. I'm an open book."

Zaria was afraid of that actually. "Quint told me about mates. How shifters grow up knowing there is that one special person out there for them, and they all want to find that person. The attraction, the pull to be together." Zaria paused to gather her thoughts. "I guess I am confused on the love part of the relationship. It's not insta-love, maybe insta-lust is more apt. Do shifters fall in love faster or easier because they accept that person is their true mate right away?"

Gerri filled two cups with coffee and handed one to her to add sugar and cream. "That is a very good question. We do know all about mates and everyone searches for theirs. Though most never find them and do settle for companionship. You are right, though, shifters know love will come with their mate so they don't second guess themselves. But for humans, you have to date someone, get to know them and hope they are the one for you. I can see your hesitation."

She sighed and fixed her drink as she thought about what Gerri said.

"Exactly, we grow up seeing movies, reading books and listening to elders talking about dating and the chess game that love is. One move forward and two back, never knowing if the person you are trying to get to know is someone worth your time or not..." Zaria trailed off and stared into space, lifting her coffee cup to her lips and taking a sip.

Did I just answer my own questions? Quint knows I'm the one for him, and I know I'm drawn to him like none other. Is that just a precursor to love? I already know I care for him and I swear I can see love shining from his eyes when he looks at me.

"Have a scone," Gerri offered.

She shook her head, her mind a whirlwind of thoughts. "No, thanks."

"I can tell you've got a lot on your mind."

Zaria glanced up at Gerri. "I guess I just need to decide if anything is keeping me attached to Earth."

Gerri sipped her coffee and put it down, taking a bite of her scone. She chewed thoughtfully before replying. "Aurora is just a portal away, you can come home anytime. I do promise Aurora promises you a lot more mane attractions."

"Very punny, but I agree. I am going to tell Quint tonight after our date, that I want to see his home on Aurora. I think I need to spend more than one night there to make sure it's the right move for me." That was it. She knew it was the right decision for her to make the best choice. No longer interested in the coffee, she slipped on her coat.

Gerri stood up at the same time she did. "Quint should be at your place soon, go have a chat. If you need to speak to me some more, remember that I'm always here for you."

Zaria hugged Gerri and headed home. There was a lot of changes coming and she just hoped she was making the right decision.

* * *

Zaria walked into her apartment, determined to take a chance she headed to her bedroom and pulled out a suitcase. *I'm going to spend some time on Aurora, so I am packing clothes. This doesn't mean it's forever. But a girl's gotta take a chance sometimes.* With that pep talk over, she packed up her clothes and put her suitcase by the front door.

Her tummy rumbled and she realized she had missed breakfast and lunch. She never did eat the scones with Gerri. She glanced at the clock, three pm so close to date time, she didn't want to fill up since she didn't know what Quint had planned.

A quick sandwich should hold her over. Or maybe she could cook dinner before their date. The old saying was the way to a man's heart was through his stomach and she was not settling for less than all his heart.

FOURTEEN

Quint had to go home to Aurora to check on Alyx and his home. He hated being away from Zaria when he was trying to make her fall in love with him. It was a forgone conclusion for him, he was falling as soon as he saw her. Then he talked to her and her sassy attitude and take-charge mindset pushed him over the edge. He loved that she knew her heart and wouldn't settle. She would keep him on his toes and it sounded perfect.

He took the time while at home to set up a few surprises, he was hedging his bets he could get her to come see his home.

Hell, he wasn't sure his dates showed her he understood some people cared about Christmas, but at least he hoped it showed her he cared about her feelings. Tonight, he planned to take her ice skating and Christmas shopping. This would be the ultimate test. Would he see humans weren't as bad as he thought or would she prove him wrong?

He shook his head, he spent a lot of time standing outside her door it seemed. Always waiting on her to open it.

"Zaria?" He knocked again a bit harder this time. "Zaria, I am coming in." He turned the door knob and walked inside. The smell of something cooking was the first thing he noticed. "I let myself in, something smells delicious. And we need to talk about my mate leaving her doors unlocked. That's not a smart move and I insist you lock the door when you are alone."

Quint walked toward the kitchen as he talked. Movement made him stop at the kitchen entrance.

"Are you really trying to tell me I can't protect myself? Hmmm? Mate or not is still up for debate, I will not have a man tell me what to do. Got it?"

"Yes, love. Do you realize you have flour on your cheek? And why are you shaking a spatula at me? Planning to spank me?" The blush that dusted her cheeks made him smile. "If you are into spanking, why didn't you say something sooner? I would be happy to accommodate that request."

Zaria backed up and put her hands in the air. "Oh no. Don't get any ideas, Quint. No spanking, just a bit of vanilla sex for me." Quint advanced on her. "You might end up liking it. I can show you a whole new world and I don't mean just Aurora."

"You're going to make me burn dinner and dessert. It's almost done, so give me just a few minutes, okay?" Zaria turned to the oven and he looked at her table. It wasn't set yet, so he started rummaging through her kitchen cabinets.

"Tell me what you're doing and I'll help you find it," she said.

"I wanted to help by setting the table, point me in the right direction, please."

Zaria stared at him with her mouth hanging open.

"What's wrong, my love?" He wondered what he'd said to shock her.

"I've never had a man help me in the kitchen before. I am shocked."

"Close your mouth, love. You have been dating the wrong kind of men. That changes now. Anyways, there will be no other men for you. I'm it." Quint couldn't help the growl that came out with those words. The thought of her looking at another drove his lion crazy.

Quint grabbed two plates from the cabinet she pointed to and set them on the table. When he turned around, she was pointing at another cabinet that held glassware. This went on a few minutes until he found everything he needed.

"What do you do for a job? Do you have one? You haven't told me much about you beyond your love of Christmas and have no young family members."

Zaria bent over to pull a roast out of the oven and Quint licked his lips. The roast smelled delicious, but the sight of her gorgeous ass bent over was what he craved. She carried it over to the table and turned back for a salad.

"I hope you like this. I don't cook a lot, but I do love to do it." He watched as she took a seat next to him, she seemed nervous and he wanted to put her at ease.

"You could've burnt everything and I would have eaten it. That's what mates do for each other."

Zaria blushed again, her beautiful gaze full of warmth. "I used to work at a local clothing store, as a manager, but they just closed down. In other words, I am actually in between jobs. I have a savings that is helping me with rent and the rest of the bills, but I need to find a job soon. I'm not stressing it. I'm good with customer service and I have a good attitude and lots of recommendations."

"When you come to Aurora, you won't need to work. If you choose to, it is all up to you. I will provide everything you need."

Zaria smirked at him. "Is that another service mates provide, hmmm?"

"Of course. I noticed you have a suitcase by the door, you weren't planning a trip without me, were you?"

Zaria licked her lips and Quint groaned. "I was going to tell you after dinner, but I guess now's a good time. I decided to come with you to Aurora for a bit to see what it's like and get to know you on your own turf."

FIFTEEN

The smile that lit up Quint's face left her breathless. His excitement over her words was palpable. He was obviously very happy she agreed to take this step with him. They started eating and talking, the meal going by pleasantly.

"I packed enough clothes for a week, if I need more we can come home pretty easily, right? I emailed all my personal information to my older sister who's the family accountant and asked her to stay on top of my bills until I come back."

"Yes, we can return pretty easily, but Aurora has some unique properties. I'm sure you saw with the dress you wore to the party? We can get you more clothes anytime. If I have my way you will stay with me forever."

"Yeah…" she licked her lips, "you mentioned that a few times. I haven't agreed yet. I just want to know more before…whatever I decide. If I do agree, I'll know what I'm getting into. I'd give up everything I know and live on another planet. I mean it's another FREAKING PLANET. That should cause any sane person a moment's pause."

"You have such a unique way of looking at things. Dinner was delicious, you relax while I clean up and then we can go out."

Zaria stared at Quint like he was an alien. Of course, he was, technically. Still, he was doing the dishes for her? Not plopping on the couch to watch football, or grabbing her and running to Aurora right away?

"Um, okay. I'm going to change. I got flour on my jeans. Do you want to eat dessert now or when we get back?"

"Hmm, after our date, love. We need to be light on our feet and I enjoyed your dinner far too much."

Zaria walked into her room, trying to decipher what light on their feet meant. Ten minutes later she was ready and so was Quint.

"I wanted to walk around the mall tonight, I need to pick up a few presents and there are some things only available on Earth. Plus, Bella begged me to bring back some chocolate for her."

Zaria was shocked he wanted to go to the mall this close to Christmas. That was one of the places he specifically said he hated. He even ranted about humans and their rude shopping tendencies. "You planned a date at the mall? I'm shocked but how does that pertain to the light on our feet you mentioned?"

Quint gave her a mischievous smile. "Well, your mall has an ice-skating rink so I thought you could drag me around a bit. Have you ever been?"

Zaria shook her head.

"Good, that means I'll have a legitimate reason to have my hands all over your body tonight." Quint smirked at her.

"This gives me a chance to get presents for Bella and the triplets, too. I'm excited, I may have to stay in Aurora through Christmas just to see the excitement on their faces. The kids' reactions is what makes the holiday so special for me. The belief in the magic that one man brings all the presents, sneaks in and leaves them behind. I love that!"

"You know we can start on our own cubs anytime. By this time next year, we can celebrate with our children opening gifts."

Zaria shook her head, "Are you trying to

convince me or yourself? I haven't agreed to anything yet." She realized she was falling in love with him, but she refused to make it easy on him. She needed to be sure this was the right move for her.

The taxi pulled up at the mall and they climbed out, Quint grabbing her hand right away. She used to think it was just a sign of possession when couples held hands. But with Quint, she just loved feeling his hand in hers. Who cared who saw them, she was content. "Are we shopping first or skating?"

Quint glanced around the area before answering. "Let's skate. It's not too busy yet and we won't have to worry about leaving any packages unattended."

Zaria walked toward the rink. "That looks really slick. Thankfully I have a lot of padding on my ass."

Quint pulled her close and wrapped his arm around her shoulder. "Don't worry, I'll rub your ass and make it feel better."

"Are you going to kiss my ass and make it better, too?" Zaria laughed at her own joke, she couldn't help it.

"Love, I will kiss every inch of your body and rub away any aches you have. Real or imagined," he whispered by her ear, placing a kiss on her jaw.

Zaria shivered and tried not to picture that in her head. A busy mall was not the place for a fantasy to play out. "Come on, let's get our skates, I can't wait to hold you close as I glide, I mean we glide across the floor. Later, I'll glide my cock into your warm wet heat."

Zaria fanned her face, trying to stop it from showing proof of her embarrassment.

"I won't have to worry about getting chilled on the ice after that. I may melt it with the heat from my body. Thanks for that." She laughed and teased him but she loved every second of his attention and his words drove her crazy.

Zaria sat on a bench and removed her shoes as she watched Quint speaking with the girl behind the counter. The bleached blonde was flirting and if she leaned over any farther her boobs would fall out of her top. Quint ignored her, tapping his fingers on the counter and looking around. She wasn't even sure he was aware she was offering him personal service.

She watched as he took the skates and walked over. The twat behind the counter stared at his ass the whole time. When he stopped she looked at Zaria and smirked. *Really? I guess I need to show you the only woman he's interested in. Showtime.* She stood up and grabbed Quint's face and pulled him down. Quint growled, dropped the skates and wrapped his arms around her waist.

She'd planned for it to be a simple kiss to show he was with her and not available. As soon as her lips touched Quint's, he growled and pulled her tight against him. Every kiss seemed a battle of the tongues but neither ever lost this war. She came to her senses a few moments later when she heard a throat being cleared.

"I think you are melting the ice my kids are skating on," said a voice filled with humor.

Zaria blushed and pulled away from Quint. She glanced over to the mom who had spoken. The woman winked at them, a friendly smile wide on her lips. "That was quite the kiss and I think you got the response you wanted."

The lady nodded her head at the counter and Zaria glanced over to see the clerk had turned her back on them.

Zaria laughed and smiled at the lady. "Thanks for the location reminder."

She noticed Quint watched the interaction with a slightly puzzled look on his face.

SIXTEEN

Quint wasn't sure he would ever understand women. They were such interesting creatures. Especially human ones. This stranger and his woman seemed to have a full conversation with only a few simple sentences. He wasn't sure what they were talking about, but he would find out later.

He sat down, pulled his boots off and put on his skates. Zaria sat down across from him and stared at her skates like they were snakes who would bite her. "Slide your foot in the skate, and I will lace them up for you. I will have a hold of you the whole time. There is nothing to be scared of."

Quint was beginning to regret his decision to

take her skating. Holding her close in public was going to test his control. The longer he was with her the more his lion begged to mate her.

"All right, my love. Let's get on the ice." Quint pulled her to her feet and walked to the rink. "The first step is the scariest, just walk like normal and I will hold you up."

Zaria stepped on the ice and smiled. "I got this, it's not so bad."

She pushed off and one leg went forward while the other went backward. Quint held her up but her face was at his waist. "While the sight of you that close to my cock is giving me quite the reaction, it's not the place, love."

He couldn't help but laugh at the face she made.

"It's just like roller skating. You've done that, right?"

With a determined look, Zaria nodded and only held on with one arm. "Let's do this. I refuse to let these kids show me up, dammit."

Quint was proud of his mate, she made it around the rink on her own after about twenty minutes of trying. She wasn't a quitter. That was a very good trait to find in his woman. Not to mention kindness. She stopped a few times to help other children who'd fallen and almost fell herself helping them on their feet.

"This was fun. Thank you for bringing me here. I think I'm done with skating, for tonight at least."

They made it around the rink one more time then stopped at the entrance to the seating area. Zaria took one stop on the carpet and dropped to her knees. Quint helped her up and growled in her ear. "If you really want to be on your knees, I can accommodate you when we get home."

Zaria flung her elbow into his stomach. "Just help me take these off. It's time for some epic shopping and you get to carry all my bags, darling."

She had a twinkle in her eye and Quint felt a bit of trepidation. He had a feeling she was going to make him pay for that last comment.

Epic shopping. Quint now knew when a woman said that to run. He was exhausted and tired of carrying bags around the mall. He loved seeing Zaria say Merry Christmas to everyone she passed by. She smiled and held doors and basically spread good cheer. Much to his surprise, every person responded in kind. She even got a few hugs from strangers. Hugs. Who hugged strangers? People who met his mate, that's who. She made quite an impression on children and older ladies especially.

The day made him realize he judged humans and their traditions too harshly.

"Zaria, are you almost done? I'm not sure I can carry one more bag," he asked, not really tired, but wanting to take her home so she could smile for him alone. Zaria turned with the evilest smile he had ever seen on a woman's face.

"We have one more stop to make and then I'll take you home and put you to bed, my man baby."

He tripped over his own feet at that. "What did you call me?"

"You heard me, man baby." Zaria's twinkling laugh caused heads to turn and check her out.

Quint had to hold back his roar of anger. "Fine, call me whatever you want. Let's just keep moving."

He stared around at the people who dared ogle his woman. He let a bit of his lion peek through and growled.

"Quint, stop it or Santa will put you on the naughty list. And we can ask him right now since that's our next stop."

He frowned at her cheerful smile. "What are you talking about, mate?"

"Every year I get my picture taken with Santa Claus. I want you to be in it this year." Quint looked up and realized they were standing in front of the store with Santa and a long line of kids who were waiting patiently for their turn.

"No. Fucking. Way."

"What?" she asked, her eyes wide.

"No way in hell. I'm not sitting on another man's lap. I love you, but you can't ask me to do that."

Zaria froze in place and Quint realized what he said. Fuck. Great timing not freaking her out and doing things slowly. "We can talk about it later. You don't have to freak out." He cleared his throat. "So, are we just cutting in front of these kids?"

She shook her head. "No. A friend of mine works here and lets me scoot in front. And you can stand next to him like I do. No laps necessary."

Quint shook his head and muttered. "The things we do for the women we love." This time Zaria only smiled. Maybe she was getting used to the idea already.

SEVENTEEN

Holy Fuck!

Breathe. Breathe. Breathe!

I can't.

He said he loved me.

I know. I'm you.

What do I do with that information? Am I ready to say it back, do I love him?

Zaria shook off her thoughts and turned to the camera. "Smile, Quint, this is painless, I promise."

This was the ultimate payback for getting her all hot and bothered in public. She really wanted to throw him to the ground and take his clothes off, but making him pose with Santa would have to do for now.

The photographer snapped a few shots and gestured to them to come see them, Quint smiled and looked only slightly in pain. Zaria pulled out her wallet, but Quint pushed her hand away.

She pouted and put her wallet away. "You could let me pay for something, Quint. I'm not broke, you know. I'm really good at budgeting my money."

He cupped her jaw and kissed her nose. "It's not a matter of having money, my love. It's me taking care of my mate. Let me spoil you now and forever."

The photographer sighed with a silly grin. "Zar, he's a keeper, babe. Don't let him go or I'll be right behind you to snatch him up."

Zaria laughed and hugged her. "Cute, Steph. I'm going out of town for a bit. I will catch up with you when I get back. If you need anything, contact Gerri Wilder and she can reach me."

Quint grabbed the bags of gifts they had purchased and watched from the edge of the crowd. With one last wave, Zaria headed toward him.

"Your smile is...infectious." He grinned back.

"Are you ready to head home now?" she

asked with mock concern, the evil twinkle in her eyes giving her away. "I'm done torturing you for tonight."

He chuckled at her words. "Torture? That's spending all night close to you but not being able to touch you. This was just exhausting. But tell me why you don't have a car. Why take a taxi everywhere?"

"I honestly didn't need one. I lived close to work and it was less money to walk or taxi anywhere. With car payments and insurance, it just wasn't worth the hassle."

"Speaking of taxi, it looks like there's one right here," he said, waving at the driver, who nodded his acknowledgment. Quint opened the door for Zaria and ran his hand down her ass as she bent to scoot in the car.

Once they got settled, she told the driver her address and Quint turned to her. "So, you are going to be away for a while, huh? How long are you planning to stay in Aurora?"

"Caught that, did ya? I forgot about shifter hearing honestly. I don't know how long I am going to stay in Aurora, but I wanted to give myself options. Steph is the only person I am really close to here." Zaria looked out the cab window. "I'm not sure I should be saying this, but

I think I'm falling in love with you." She closed her eyes for a second, blocking out reality before opening them to the colorful street lights. "But there are still so many variables to consider. I need to see what it's like there and if I can live there before I take that leap with you."

Quint took her hand in his. "Love, I will live here if that's what you want. All I need is you, no matter where that is."

Tears stung Zaria's eyes. He made it all sound so easy. How could she ask him to give up his home, family and friends to spend his life on Earth? A place he didn't really enjoy. One day he would end up resenting her for it. She wasn't willing to take that chance. Aurora would be their only option, so it was time to really consider if she could handle this change.

Steeling her spine and accepting the chance she was taking, she met his gaze. "Can we leave first thing in the morning? Will it be hard to bring all these gifts and my suitcase?"

Zaria glanced at the taxi driver who kept looking at them in the rearview mirror. He had the strangest look on his face, he must have heard part of the conversation.

"We can go right now if you want. My home is always open for you, and I know Bella would give you a room in the palace if you wanted it instead."

Zaria thought about it for a minute. "The morning is fine. I'm tired and I just want to enjoy one last night in my bed before everything changes."

The taxi pulled up at her apartment and Quint once again refused to allow her to pay. "Come on, love. Let's get upstairs and into bed. I just want to hold you tonight."

God. The things he said. Was he real? This man was so sweet and kind. He was one of a kind. Not many men would be willing to just go to sleep after all the teasing they had shared all day long. Her heart thudded hard and a flood of an emotion she'd never experienced before filled her chest. He made it easier and easier to fall in love with him. *Are you sure you're not in love already?* Was she? That could be dangerous if things didn't work out. She had to hope she could come out the other side with her heart intact.

* * *

Zaria looked around, her excitement mounting over spending more time in this beautiful planet. "I can't believe how easy it is to travel to Aurora and the beauty of this planet. I almost had myself convinced I made up the colors."

His chest puffed out, pride evident in his

gaze. "Earth is pretty, but it lacks the color you see here. I think only a few places on Earth could compare."

They walked farther from the castle, but she could still see it was pretty close. "This planet is gorgeous."

"Are you ready to see my home? It's just around this corner. When I came home yesterday, I made sure you would be comfortable here." He smiled at her and held her hand as they walked.

"Pretty confident in yourself, huh?" Zaria couldn't resist the man when he smiled. His whole face lit up, and her pussy clenched in need.

They walked a bit farther and his house came into view. She stopped dead in her tracks, a soft gasp rushing out of her. "Oh, my."

"Is that a good thing?" he asked, worry in his tense stance.

"I never thought about my dream home before, but I think this is it."

He lived in a log cabin, but rustic it was not. It had a wide wraparound porch with rocking chairs and a swing. The lake he mentioned was not far away and the view was incredible. She could see snow-capped mountains in the distance. "If the inside is as gorgeous as the outside, you will have to drag me away from here."

EIGHTEEN

Quint was excited to show Zaria the surprises he had in store for her. The first of which was sitting inside waiting on her to walk in. "Door's open, love, just go on in." He watched as she went up the three steps to his front door.

Zaria opened the door and stepped inside and stopped. "Quint, what is all of this?"

An unnatural insecurity came over him. Did she like it? Would she take this and make it her new home? Fuck! Would she stay?

"I didn't want you to think you were leaving all your traditions behind. I went out yesterday and found a tree, then my mom helped me find the decorations from a trip she took a few years ago." He stopped behind her, his gaze roaming the stuff he'd placed there. "The boxes are full of everything you could possibly want to decorate the tree and even the outside of the house. I know living in an apartment you probably didn't have that ability so, I hoped you would decorate our house."

Zaria turned around and stared at him. "Our house?" She grinned and the cold vice around his stomach disappeared. "I love the sound of that. Can we start the tree now? I am so excited!"

"Actually, I was hoping you would take a walk with me. I wanted to show you more of Aurora before it got too dark to see much. There's a small town center not far away. I wanted to take you there."

"Sure, that sounds great. Where can I put my stuff?" She lowered her gaze and shifted from foot to foot before glancing up and smiling softly. "I mean, am I sleeping in your room?"

The fact she'd even thought for a nano-second that she might not was adorable. "If I have my way, mate, you will never leave my bed again." He hugged and kissed her. The house finally felt like a home with his mate in it. He was ready to live the life he was meant to, with her by his side. "My lion agrees one hundred percent. My room is down the hall. We'll leave your stuff in there and we can go."

"I'll go. Give me a second," she cleared her

throat and stared at him with lust-filled eyes. "If we both go in there, we might not come out for a while."

"You read my mind."

She laughed and shook her head, pulling her rolling suitcase down the hall. "No, I read my own mind. And right now, it's very, very dirty."

Quint watched her walk away and he fought for control over his lion. Having Zaria in his home, near his bed was driving both of them crazy. His lion pushed to mate her now and keep her until she accepted them. He turned away from her retreating form and looked out the window. Distraction was what he needed, otherwise he would follow her down the hall and toss her on the bed. Then fuck her until she begged for him to mate her and make her his forever.

"Quint, are you okay? I can hear you growling down the hall." Zaria moved closer, the heat of her body against his back making his blood thicken.

"I'm fine. Let's go before I change my mind." He turned from the window and walked out front of the house. When Zaria didn't follow, he looked back over his shoulder. She stood in the doorway with her arms wrapped around her waist, her eyes filled with tears.

"What happened? What upset you?" Quint looked all around them, trying to figure out what happened in those seconds.

"Before you change your mind?" Zaria whispered, her voice cracking. "You want me to go back to Earth already?"

Fuck. His shortness had given her the wrong impression. He stalked up to her and slammed his lips over hers. "I told you. I am never letting you go. I wanted to drag you into the bedroom and fuck you into the mattress, until your scent permeated every inch of my bedroom. I wanted you begging me to mate you and writhing under me in pleasure. But I said we would go on a walk and we will." He licked the seam of her lips. "That's why we have to go. Because I don't want you to feel like you're only here for sex. I want us to bond."

He stepped back and held his hand out to Zaria. She stood there, licking her lips and staring at him with lust etched into every feature. "I think I like the idea of skipping a walk right now."

"I have another surprise for you. I don't want to ruin it. Please come with me and then I promise to let you ride my cock as long as you want tonight." Quint growled the words softly, but knew they left an impact. She visibly shook as she put her hand in his.

Her gaze held his. "Take me."

Quint hung his head. "You play dirty, mate."

His woman was a lot in a small human package. She was so much more than he ever expected or thought to find. Fate was kind to him and he could never give enough thanks for finding his true mate.

"It's about a quarter mile walk through the woods. Are you okay to walk that far, love?" Distraction was the name of the game with Zaria. Otherwise he didn't think he would ever get anything done.

Zaria snorted, matching his strides. "Of course. Lead the way, my lion in shining armor. Tell me about this town area you're taking me to. This is so fun. I love playing tourist."

He chuckled at her excitement. She was adorable. Like a curious child. "I call it a town, but really it's just a few dozen families who built their homes fairly close together. Over time, they have taken on aspects of a small town, one family bakes and trades goods with the others. Others farm and trade their goods. Each family has something to offer and they are pretty self-sufficient. Of course, they are mostly lions, there are a couple other shifters in the mix but not many. After all, most of the people closest to the castle are part of Alyx's pride."

"That sounds fascinating. I can't wait to see it. Is there a common area or just a bunch of houses in a small area?"

"They built a town center. It's where they meet to trade items and hang out. That's where we, my beauty, are headed."

Quint watched Zaria as they walked through the woods, her smile and curious glances here and there, oohing and aahing, made him see the forest as if for the first time. He spent so much time there he forgot how pretty the trees, flowers and odd the creatures could be. A life with Zaria would bring so many new experiences and open his eyes to his world all over again. It was true what he'd heard elders say: you overlook that which you see every day.

"Zaria, the town area I was telling you about is just beyond these trees." Quint hoped she would be excited with his next surprise. Convincing the families to help him was a feat in itself. Hopefully they would have fun and not make him regret asking.

They marched through the trees. He saw the first few houses. Children played outside and adults gathered in groups, talking and going about their day. When they spotted Zaria, the conversations tapered off until they all were staring.

"Quint, I'm getting nervous. Why are they staring at me?" she whispered in a hushed panic.

"I told them I was bringing my mate and they're checking you out. Don't worry, beautiful. Just be yourself. They will love you as much as I do."

Zaria kept walking, smiling and nodding at everyone as she caught their eye. He was so proud of her. He could sense her concern and hesitation, but she took everything in stride. From the staring to the warm hellos. Thankfully, everyone was nice and welcoming. As they reached the center of the town, she stopped and turned around.

"This is Zaria, my mate. Zaria, this everyone. They will take turns introducing themselves so they don't overwhelm you all at once. Don't worry. You won't be expected to remember who is who right away either."

One of the lionesses around Zaria's age made her way over. With long red hair and peachy skin, she was a beauty. But her emerald green eyes made her stand out in the crowd. Not the color of her eyes. The genuine warmth in them. He noticed the tension in his mate immediately eased as the lioness came closer.

"Hi, I'm Dalissa. I'm *so* excited to meet you. I have never been to Earth but always wanted to go. Would you mind if I asked you a million questions?"

Zaria laughed at Dalissa's excitement over

Earth. Quint grinned. It had been the same excitement she'd experienced over Aurora. In the blink of an eye, she started chatting with Dalissa. The rest of the people gathered went back to their conversations. He stood next to her and just listened in, she needed to connect with them if she wanted to stay. Hopefully this would help cement her desire to stay in Aurora.

After a few minutes, when it looked like Dalissa was getting the most out of her interview of his mate, Quint kissed the side of Zaria's head and whispered, "I'll be right back."

NINETEEN

Zaria watched Quint walk away and sighed.

"Girl, you got it bad," Dalissa laughed. "I know that look. It's so cute how in love you are with him. And I mean LOVE with a capital L."

She glanced at Dalissa, a smile lifting her lips. "Am I that obvious?"

"We are going to be the bestest of friends. I know it," she assured her with so much conviction Zaria believed it, too. "So, I'm going to tell you the truth in terms you can understand. You're human. You are like those cartoons they tell us human kids grow up watching. You know the ones where the hearts float above their heads and their eyes turn into heart shapes?" She gave a firm nod. "Yes. That's you. By the way, that is weird as shit stuff to allow kids to watch."

Zaria could barely stop laughing. Dalissa was hilariously honest and real. She loved her. She knew exactly what Dalissa referred to. It seemed normal to her, but she understood how it would look odd to someone not used to Earth's standards. Someone called Dalissa's name and she looked away and then back for a second.

"Don't go anywhere," Dalissa said with a smile. "I'll be right back. We have so much more to talk about."

She was alone a second before she heard a voice at her back. "Why don't you go back to Earth where you belong? You humans come here and take all the good men."

Zaria whirled around to see a stunning woman standing behind her. "Excuse me?" She blinked in disbelief at the beautiful woman. Like she could have a hard time getting a man. "Maybe your men wouldn't need to find women on Earth if they found mates here. If you were their mates, they wouldn't keep looking, now would they?"

Her cold stare made Zaria tense, but she wasn't one to show fear. If she backed away now, others would think her a coward.

The woman's eyes glowed angry gold. "We can still be together, mates or not. I'm sick and tired of you humans taking what doesn't belong to you. Watch your back and tell that Bella bitch to watch out for hers, too. She took our king. His duty was to mate one of ours. To keep Aurora pure. Not mixing our bloodlines with weak human DNA. I'm not the only one who isn't happy Aurora is getting filled with Earth whores."

"Whore? I'd watch who you call a whore," Zaria snapped. "Bella's my friend. She's the queen of this planet and if you don't like it, too fucking bad." She glared at the lioness. "I bet the king would love to know how you feel."

The lioness hissed some colorful words and stomped away. Zaria stared in shock. Did Quint know this was going on under his nose? Fuck, Bella and the triplets, they needed to be protected at all costs. Zaria spun around searching for Quint, she had to tell him right away.

"Zaria," Dalissa rushed up to her side. "What's wrong? You look as white as snow. What happened? I was only gone for a minute."

Zaria grabbed Dalissa's hands. "Thank god you came back. I need to find Quint right away. Can you see him anywhere? Or do you know where he is?"

"I don't, but let's go look for him. I'll have your back," Dalissa said with a somber tone.

They searched for Quint for long, tense minutes. Then, finally, Dalissa yelled out, "There he is!" She pointed and called out to a group of men. "Quint, come here quickly. Zaria is upset and needs you."

Quint emerged from the group, his scowl deep and set. He marched quickly to them. "What happened? Are you okay?"

He grabbed her hands and scanned her body for bruises or injuries.

Zaria sighed and threw her arms around him, needing the contact. "I'm fine, physically. This woman came up behind me and started yelling at me about us humans taking away the men and how we should stay on Earth. I said if they could find their mates here they wouldn't go to Earth to get them. Then she told me to watch my back and Bella should, too."

Reliving the words and the venom with which they'd been said was too much. Her gut twisted in knots and tears burned the back of her eyes. She pulled away, not wanting him to think her weak.

"Zaria," Quint growled, fear and worry in his eyes.

She shook her head and wiped the tears from her cheeks. "I'm sorry. I hate that I cry when I'm angry. I'm pissed for my friend, not afraid for myself. I'm worried for Bella and the babies. Why would she wait this long to threaten Bella?"

Quint pulled her into his chest, with his arms around her body she felt invincible. Nothing would ever hurt her. He kissed her and then met her gaze. "We need to go to the palace to let Alyx know what happened. Did you get her name?"

"Fuck! She didn't offer it and I didn't ask, I was too pissed at what she was saying honestly. I wasn't very nice either." Zaria mentally yelled at herself for not asking her name.

"Quint," Dalissa interjected, "I saw Bet'any stomping away. It could've been her. She has been acting strange lately. I heard mutterings of an anti-human group that was going around trying to recruit members."

Zaria couldn't believe what she was hearing. He was asking her to move to a planet that now had an anti-human group. There were so few on Aurora that she'd be an easy target. That was not what she was signing up for. She glanced at Quint and memorized his face. There was a lot more to think about now. She had to go to the palace to make sure Bella was safe and the babies.

Common sense rushed back at that moment. What was she doing on a planet where she wasn't wanted? At least on Earth, she'd be part of the majority. In Aurora, she'd be in danger. Quint would have to be her constant bodyguard and she wasn't looking for a babysitter. This had been a nice idea, but not the best action with the current issues rising in Aurora. She needed to go home. She didn't belong there and this proved it.

Quint swore and roared. "If anyone here is harboring anti-human ideas, you need to leave now and run. Our queen is human. Many of our mates are human. Get as far the fuck away as possible. We will hunt you down and there will be no mercy." The group around them started muttering to themselves and looking at each other. He took her hand and squeezed. "Come on. We need to get to the palace right away."

From the crowd stepped out an older man. "Take my transport bike. It would be my honor to help you today."

Quint nodded his head and guided her along.

Transport bike? That sounded like a motorcycle, but something told her it was a different type of bike. As they walked toward the man, he tossed a key to Quint, which he caught easily. Then they walked past him and around the back of one of the houses.

She gasped, her eyes wide. The transport bike, well, had no wheels at all! It was a tripod base, but it looked like a padded appendage at the bottom. More like three of them. The top was covered with a glass-like dome and it opened on either side. Quint walked to the closest side and slid in. "Come to the other side and slide in behind me."

She bit her lip and shook her head as she did what he told her. *Snap out of it, Zaria. Now is not the time for innuendoes.* She sat down and wrapped her arms around Quint's waist. "How fast does this go and how do you swerve around the trees and debris on the ground?"

Quint smirked over his shoulder. "Did I mention we're flying? No obstacles to worry about."

The world shifted and for a second she worried she'd pass out. She squeezed Quint's waist tightly and buried her head in his back. "I forgot to mention, I get motion sick."

He patted the hands she'd wrapped around his waist. "This will be over quickly, mate. Just hold on and I will take you out another time to enjoy Aurora from the sky."

Within seconds they were airborne. Wind rushed through her hair, but she wasn't looking up to see how high they were. She focused on Quint's warm scent and the stomach muscles contracting as she held on tight. He was right, though, the flight was over quickly. With barely a jolt, the bike touched down and she finally looked up. The palace was right in front of them, and Alyx was waiting on them.

"Dalissa called to warn us you were coming with urgent news. She mentioned you had brought Zaria back with you. Bella's in my office waiting on us all."

Quint helped Zaria off the bike and she was pleased to note, her legs were steady. Even if her heart was still pounding a mile a minute. Quint held onto her hand as they walked into the palace and to Alyx's office. As soon as they walked in, Bella rushed over and wrapped her arms around her.

"Zaria, I am so happy you came back to Aurora so fast!" She nodded to their joined hands, "Does these mean you are mated?"

Zaria jumped and dropped Quint's hand. "No, we aren't mated. Though he says I'm his. But we aren't here about that, Bella." Zaria looked up at Quint and stopped speaking. He should tell them what happened. It was their people and their world, not hers. She was just an interloper like that woman implied.

Zaria walked over to the couch across from Alyx's desk and sat down. Bella sat close to her and wrapped her arm around Zaria's shoulders.

TWENTY

Fuck, she's pulling away from me. I can feel it and see it in her eyes. He didn't have time to deal with that right now. Her safety and that of the other humans on Aurora had to be secured first.

He took a deep breath and walked closer to Alyx's desk. "A woman who lives in the town just past my place had a few interesting words for Zaria today." Quint glanced over at her to see how she was doing. "She said the humans are taking away the men and they had to watch their backs."

From across the room Zaria spoke up. "I told her if you had found your mates here, then you wouldn't have come to Earth, but she didn't care." Zaria turned on the couch to face Bella.

"She said I had to watch my back and to tell you to watch yours."

Alyx roared across the room and Karel, his first in command, came rushing into the room. "What happened?"

Quint watched Alyx's best friend scan the room for any threat and slowly relax.

"Apparently there is a faction of shifters who feel we need to stop going to Earth to find mates. They're going around trying to get more followers. They threatened my mate and Alyx's. I imagine any and all humans on Aurora need to be warned."

Karel, who had a human mate, growled in response. "Let's go hunting."

Alyx took control of the situation immediately. "Karel, get a hold of Brecc and Eros, Viktor and Talen, let them know their mates are in danger. And send someone you trust to get Aliva and bring her here, she can stay with Bella and Zaria. Same goes for Charlotte, Rebecca and Cassie. We can assume the heads of each clan will be descending on us soon to find out what is going on and how far it reaches."

As Karel stalked out of the room yelling for the soldiers, Zaria whispered to Bella. "Who are all those people?"

"Mates. Karel is Alyx's right hand man and

he is mated to a human named Aliva. Brecc and Eros are wolves and mated to another human, Charlotte."

"Hot damn! Lucky bitch gets two?" Zaria gasped.

Bella laughed at Zaria and Quint frowned at them.

"Viktor is a dragon and mated to Rebecca, also human. Lastly Talen, a bear, is mated to Cassie. Another human," Bella finished.

"Did you say dragon?" Zaria squealed. "Like a real freaking dragon? Why didn't anyone tell me there were dragons here?" She shook her head. "Never mind, those are questions for another time."

Quint was happy to see she seemed to be out of her funk from earlier. "Alyx, I'm going to take Zaria with me while you plan with Quint. When the other women arrive, send them to the nursery, please. I need to be close to the babies."

Quint watched them walk out of the room. Zaria never looked at him. "Dammit, Alyx. She's pulling away. I brought her here to show her she could be happy here. She's my mate, but she says mate doesn't necessarily mean love. I can't lose her. We need to wrap this up quickly. She'll run otherwise. I just know it."

Alyx marched over to his side and put his

hand on Quint's shoulder. "We'll do our best. Bella won't let her go easily. She can see you belong together."

Alyx was right but it hurt to let her walk out and not chase her down. "Now tell me who the woman was who threatened our mates."

"If Dalissa was right, her name is Bet'any. I'm confused because she's not a troublemaker. She's always been fairly quiet. I don't know her well, just a passing hello when I was passing through. Dalissa said she heard rumors of an anti-human group that was recruiting, but she didn't know anymore." He growled and combed his fingers through his hair. "I should have asked for more information, but I wanted to warn you and the others right away."

The door behind them burst open and in walked Brecc, Eros, Viktor, Talen and Karel.

Alyx raised his brows. "Damn, that was fast."

Brecc, Eros and Viktor shrugged and Talen just smiled. No one was bothering to explain how fast they got there and frankly Quint didn't care.

"Quint, catch them up really quick, please." Alyx walked over and shut the door and Quint filled them in. "Are the women with Bella and Zaria?"

The men all nodded and Karel spoke up. "It

sounds like we need to make a trip to this village." Quint nodded in agreement. They needed to flush out the culprits. "I will defer to you Alyx or Karel, these are your people to lead."

Brecc frowned at Eros. "You go with them to the town or village, whatever it is. I'm heading back home to ask around to see if anyone has tried recruiting in the wolf packs."

They all turned to Viktor and Talen to see what they were thinking.

Viktor spoke first. "I'll come with you to the town and then on home to check with my people."

Talen nodded. "Good idea. I'll do the same. We need to see how far reaching this is before we take action."

Quint followed as they turned and walked out of the room. He had to be honest, if this group of men was coming for him, he would be running like hell. Like him, they were scary as fuck. He could take them one on one, but as a group, a person would be stupid to do that. None of them would put up with anyone threatening their mates or their people.

Along with Alyx, these men led their packs, clans and friends with dignity and courage. Quint wasn't stupid enough to underestimate them. He felt sorry for the idiots who'd come up with an anti-human group. They'd live to regret it. Until they were dead.

TWENTY-ONE

Zaria sat in the nursery watching the women talk about Aurora and their friends in each pack. She knew it was another world, but she felt separated from them. They weren't even scared of the threat.

They were so confident it would be fine. They said their men would handle it and there was nothing to do but catch up with each other. She watched as Bella put each toddler to sleep and tiptoed back to them. "Let's go sit somewhere else. I asked for Sidaii wine to be sent to us and to keep it coming. Rooms are being made up for each of you, too."

Liv jumped up first. "Hell yeah, bring on the wine!"

Cassie seemed the quietest of the bunch, or maybe she was just that way around new people. She quickly followed Liv out of the room. Charlotte grabbed Rebecca and pulled her up from the couch, which left Bella staring at her.

"Come on, some wine and gossip will do you some good tonight. We really are safe here. At one time I'd be paranoid, but I trust these men, Zaria. All our men. They're strong, diligent and can be a person's worst nightmare when they threaten their loved ones. They will have this handled in no time at all."

Zaria sighed and got up. Wine did sound good and if there was gossip, she was totally going to ask Rebecca about being mated to two men. She better be ready to share some juicy details.

Bella led them to a sitting room. It looked like a living room to her, but it was a palace so better names and all that. Cassie went straight for the wine and started pouring everyone a glass.

"A toast to old friends and new friends." All the women turned to Zaria and smiled. Charlotte continued the toast. "To our mates, who will always protect us, love us and still need to learn we are capable of taking care of ourselves." As one, the women laughed and yelled. "Cheers".

Liv sat down next to Zaria and turned to look at her "All right, spill the beans. How did you meet Quint? Why haven't you mated him?"

Bella shushed her. "Zaria, you don't have to answer her, but we are here if you need to talk. We have all been through similar shit when we first found we were mated to shifters. We could tell you stories of the shit they did. Especially Brecc and Eros and a case of kidnapping. They always mean well but don't necessarily think about how stuff comes across to us humans."

Zaria gaped at Bella and then looked at the other women. They were all laughing and shaking their heads. She took a deep breath. If these women couldn't help her then there was no hope. They at least understood where she was coming from. She opened her mouth to start and Cassie jumped up.

"Just a minute, let me fill our glasses and bring the wine closer."

Zaria glanced down at her glass and was shocked to realize she'd drank the whole thing already. At this rate she'd be a lush before she got her questions answered.

Cassie filled the glasses, Rebecca made a toast this time. Then they all turned and stared at her, ready to hear what she had to say. Zaria picked up her glass and drained it, she needed liquid courage right now. "My first and biggest problem is this whole insta-mate business. That doesn't mean insta-love, right?"

They all nodded their heads a resounding yes. Well, shit.

Cassie leaned over and patted her hand. "We get it, they grow up knowing about their ONE, but to us, it's still a lottery."

Zaria was thrilled they understood her. She took another sip of her wine, *when the hell did that get refilled for the third or fourth time?* She shook the thought off. That wasn't important. "So, yeah, wasn't it hard to just leave everything behind on Earth to move to another planet with a shifter? I mean we knew they existed but most of us had never met one, then boom, I'm mated to one and he wants me to have cubs and move to another planet. Come on, is he serious with this shit?"

Zaria stopped talking when she realized she had just word vomited all over them. Thankfully they all wore looks of sympathy. Zaria picked up her wine glass and Liv quickly filled it up again.

"Thanks," she mumbled.

"Tell us how you really feel," Bella grinned with a wink.

"Dammit, I love that man and I want to stay." Zaria froze when she realized what she'd said. Out loud.

"Are you just realizing you love him, Zaria?" She wasn't sure which woman had asked that, and when the hell did they become twins? Oh, for fuck's sake, she was seeing doubles now!

"Uh…yeah. I mean I knew I was attracted to him. The sex is mind-blowing, but I wanted to be sure it was love before I agreed to anything, you know?" God. It took alien wine to make her realize she loved an alien shifter and his alien god-like cock.

Bella laughed. "Yes, the sex can be quite mind-blowing. Want to know a secret?" she whispered loudly. "It only gets better after you're mated, though. I'm pretty sure I heard him call you love a couple times, right?"

"So, it's your love you were questioning?" Charlotte asked.

Zaria squinted over at Charlotte. She nodded slowly to keep herself from falling sideways. "Yes, I've been doubting myself. My closest friend was Bella and she moved away. My family members are all older and we aren't as close as we once were. I'm thirty-five and the youngest daughter. My nieces and nephews are off doing their own thing. Everyone's off living their new adult life. Doing things they always wanted to do and are too busy for gatherings and, well, me." She sucked down more wine. "I didn't realize how lonely I've been until now. God, I sound like a fucking loser. I want a family already. My own family. Anyway, now that I've shown how pathetic my life is, tell me about your yummy men sandwich."

Cassie bounced in her seat, her face flushed and her eyes dancing with joy. "Have you seen Brecc and Eros? How do you know they're yummy?"

Zaria laughed so hard she couldn't stop the tears. Cassie was adorable and definitely crazy in love with her bear. Who would've thought it was possible? "Every man on Aurora is stunning. It was a safe assumption."

Charlotte leaned forward and almost fell out of her seat. "I will tell you, if you tell us...are you staying or are you running? We all know you were thinking about it when we walked in here."

It took her a moment of foggy thinking, but she realized they'd gotten her drunk on purposed. "You bitches suck. I'll probably hate you all tomorrow for filling my glass so much, but I'm staying." She shook her finger at Bella. "Nope. Don't look at me like that. I'm staying here with my mane cock," she giggled. "Get it. Oh, man. That Sidaii wine is bad news. Now get on with it. I need to hear all about it. She turned to Cassie next. "I want to know about you and your bear love." Then she peeked at Rebecca in awe. "Holy fuck, girl, a dragon? I mean are they all bigger than average because of their animals? I thought I won a prize with Lion Goldencock, but y'all got me wondering."

Bella laughed until she sputtered, her face red. "Are you really asking about the size of their mates' cocks?"

"Did you really call Quint Lion Goldencock?" Rebecca giggled.

Zaria nodded her head so fast the room started to spin. The last thing she heard was laughter.

TWENTY-TWO

A few hours after the men left to go to town, the men met up in Alyx's office again. Quint paced back and forth waiting on them to report back in and update everyone. When they got to the little town, Bet'any was sitting on a table in the main area. She'd been waiting on them patiently.

After being surrounded by six angry alphas, she spilled everything she knew. A few older women and men who hadn't found their mates yet were upset that their leaders were looking outside of Aurora for a mate and decided to try and lead a rebellion. It was really sad, they had five members including Bet'any. She denied reaching out to the other shifters, but the others were checking to be sure.

All five were contained in the palace until Alyx could decide their fate and make sure the whole thing was as small as she claimed.

Brecc marched in first and glanced over at Eros. He gave a brief nod and a quick grin. Quint took that as all was well with the wolves. He had to admit it must be handy to communicate directly with someone without the aid of technology.

Brecc walked over to stand next to Eros and they all turned to stare at the door. Viktor and Talen were still checking on their clans. When the door opened, they all straightened up and focused when one of Alyx's personal butlers, Gregory, walked in.

"Sir, I went to check on the ladies as you asked." Gregory fidgeted and looked unsure if he should continue speaking."

"Go on," Alyx said in a no-nonsense tone.

"Well, they're passed out," Gregory said with surprise. "All of them."

Alyx roared and jumped to his feet, Karel started running to the door with Brecc, Eros and Quint on his heels.

"Wait!" Gregory yelled. "It's nothing bad, sir. There were several jugs of Sidaii wine next to them," he gulped. "Sir, I think they got drunk."

Karel was the first to start laughing and they

all followed suit. Quint was relieved. His mate needed to relax and hopefully, the ladies put her fears to rest. He couldn't wait much longer to mate her. His lion wasn't happy and was pushing constantly now.

Viktor and Talen walked in and stared at them with confusion. Quint tried to stop laughing so he could explain. Eros was finally able to share the news.

"Well, that was unexpected news," Viktor chuckled. He'd become a much more tolerable dragon since he mated Rebecca. "I assume we have guest rooms available, there is no way I am flying Rebecca home on my back when she is passed out."

Alyx waved his hand at Viktor with a grin. "Of course, now tell us what you found out, please." Viktor shook his head "No one had heard anything of these rumblings. My dragons are not involved."

"Nor are the bears," Karel added. "They were upset anyone threatened my mate. I don't see this being a problem for long."

Quint stood up from the couch he'd settled on. "This could've gone really badly. I mean, really badly. With this good news, how about we gather our women and get them to bed. I have a mate to claim when she sobers up."

As a group, they all headed to the sitting room that Bella loved to use. Inside they found Liv laid across Zaria's lap, Zaria leaning against the side of the couch, and across from them on the other couch were Rebecca and Charlotte. It was hard to say who was holding who up between those two. Bella and Cassie sat in chairs on either side of the coffee table. Well, Cassie sat in the chair. Bella was almost on the floor.

"Anyone else get the idea these women will be wanting to spend a lot more time together? Somehow, I feel it could be very dangerous for us, too," Eros said to no one in particular.

Quint laughed at the fear in Eros' voice. He was right, though. These women could move mountains if they tried. Together they were a force to be reckoned with.

"Goodnight, gentlemen. I'm going to untangle my mate and put her to bed," Karel said with a chuckle.

Quint wanted to grab Zaria and hold her close but he had to wait until Karel could pull his mate off of her.

* * *

The next morning, Quint stood by the window in their guest room when he heard a moaning from behind him. He grinned, knowing she was probably wishing she'd stopped at one glass of Sidaii. "Good morning, mate. Thank you for not running last night."

Zaria groaned again and Quint chuckled. "Ouch. Did you carry me to bed? I don't remember much after we talked about your cocks."

Quint raised an eyebrow at her, his complete focus on her words. He offered her glass of water. "You talked about what?"

She grimaced and took the glass of water and drank it before replying. "Well, I think we joked. I'm not sure we actually said anything. I think we passed out too fast. Anyways, how did you know I was going to run?"

After she drank the water, he refilled the glass and passed it to her again, watching her sip at a slower pace. "It was all over your face and body language. What made you change your mind?"

She finished the water and put the glass on the nightstand. Then she climbed out of bed and walked to the desk in the corner of the room. "Is this coffee? It smells like coffee."

Quint growled at her "It's like coffee. Now answer me, dammit."

She gave him her back as she poured a cup. "It's simple. I realized I love you."

Quint stalked over to her and turned her around. "You can't say that and not look me in the eye."

Zaria had the most dazzling smile he'd ever seen on any female. "I love you. That's all that matters. Now make me yours forever, please."

Quint leaned down and kissed her. "God, Zaria. I've been waiting to hear you say that. I love you, too."

He kissed her again. The kiss broke for all of a second before their lips were once again pressed together, tongues rubbing and breaths mingling. She gripped his shirt in her hands and tugged it up. Quint pulled it off and tugged on hers, he put her to bed last night in just a t-shirt and underwear. He was thankful for that small victory today. He kissed his way down her neck, across her breasts and to her stomach as he pushed her back to the bed.

"Lean back on the bed for me, love."

Zaria didn't hesitate as he took her nightgown off. He kissed his way up her leg until he breathed over her clit and glanced at her. "I've never wanted to watch my dick go in and out of a pussy as badly as I do now. Yours."

He took a feather-light swipe of her clit with his tongue, enough to get her to lift her ass off the bed, ready to bring her sex to his lips.

"To listen to you moan. To feel your pussy grip my cock." He placed a kiss on her mound. "To come inside you and fill you with my cum. Ah, baby. I want you full with my offspring. I want you full of me." He rubbed a finger around her entrance, driving her mindless with need. "I've never wanted anything so much, Zaria. Never have I wanted a woman like I want you." He sucked in a breath.

"Your pussy's begging me to fuck it. Begging me to slide deep and make you mine. Asking me with each grip to pound you so hard, you're left incapable of walking. Incapable of talking. Unable to fucking breathe."

TWENTY-THREE

She choked on the air struggling into her lungs. "Do it." She bit her lips and gripped his hair tightly. "I want your tongue inside me. I want you to make me scream. Make me come. Please, Quint."

She hadn't finished saying his name when he dropped his head farther and did a long, slow lick from ass to clit.

Her back arched, and her belly quivered from the lightning bolts rushing through her. He licked at her folds, groaning and rumbling. Her grip on his hair didn't loosen. Her legs trembled. Need grew in her core, twining the rope of tension that would bring her release. Another swipe of his tongue and she saw stars. He lapped at her pussy, growling and snarling with every drive of his tongue into her.

"Good god!"

His arms curled around her legs, holding her shaking thighs open and keeping her from squeezing them closed on his head. His nose pressed on her clit, rubbing it side to side and pushing her just over the edge she was desperate to leap from.

She screamed so loud she swore others must've heard her. Pleasure swept through her, cooling the aching heat and taming the desperate yearning to have him inside. For a second.

Her legs shook hard. He stood, his face wet with her orgasm. He licked his lips, and the lust riding her took control again. She scraped her nails on his arms, pulling him close for a kiss. He gave it. Hard. Fast. Then he pulled her off the bed and had her turn around to lay her upper body over it.

He caressed her back down to her ass and growled. "You have a beautiful ass." She glanced over her shoulder, watching him lick his lips again and stare at her cheeks like they were a meal.

He pressed his erection between her cheeks, and she forgot all about it. Her mind focused on wanting him to fuck her.

"Quint, god," she mumbled. He leaned forward, pressing his dick harder on her ass and grabbing clumps of her hair to tug her head back.

"I need you, Zaria. I want inside you." The words were low, rough, and almost unintelligible.

Thank fuck! She was ready to get on her knees and beg. He pulled away, and she felt the material of his pants sliding down the back of her legs. Then he grabbed her hips and hauled her rear up, pressing the head of his dick into her entrance. She was soaking wet and more turned on than from using her vibrators twice in a row.

With a single-minded thrust, he plunged deeply into her, stretching her pussy muscles to the limit.

"Oh, yesss," she hissed.

She leaned harder on the desk, scraping her nails on the surface and looking for something to cling to. He yanked on her hair, tugging her head toward him, and placed kisses on her slick spine. "Do you know how fucking hot it is that your pussy is clamping tightly around my dick?"

She blinked at the haze clouding her vision. "Tell me."

"Every time," he grunted, pulling out and driving forth. "I slide into your wet heat," he bit on her shoulder and thrust hard, making her get on her tiptoes. He dug his hand into her hip and fucked her with increasing speed. "I want to feel that suction your pussy does when you come." He rubbed his chin on the side of her neck. "Tell me you want this. Tell me." She glanced over her shoulder, looking for his lips. A deep dive and his face came close to brush his lips with hers. She panted for air.

"I want this. I want you. I want us. Forever. Now fuck me. Do it. However you want." She licked her lips and glanced at his mouth then at his deep, shifting eyes. He plunged once, twice, and stopped, biting on the back of her shoulder. A scream tore through her.

Her shoulder felt aflame. He scraped his nails from the front to the back of her hips, adding to the combination of pleasure and pain she experienced. He roared and let go of her hair. Both his hands squeezed her hips as he plunged fast into her; she slid back and forth on the desk thanks to the perspiration all over her chest.

She gasped, unable to say anything. He thrust in and out of her in quick, harsh slides. Her pussy grasped at his shaft. She felt her channel clench tightly around him as her orgasm flowed through her.

"Quint," she whimpered.

Her pussy gripped him so hard it was painful. Her channel contracted like never before, then it cooled. Tides of pleasure cascaded over her burning muscles, leaving her feeling lax and weightless.

Quint roared louder than she'd ever thought possible. His nails dug into her hips. His cock thickened inside her, spilling his semen and filling her with his heat.

He laid down next to her and pulled her boneless body atop of him, so he was on his back and she was laying on his chest. "You were right, being mates doesn't make us perfect or an automatic couple. My love for you does. Thank you for being patient with me, and helping me see how amazing you really are. I love you forever and a day."

Zaria lifted her head off Quint's chest, with tears running down her face. "Thank you for being patient enough to show me what true mates could be. Nothing could have prepared me for your love, but I will never let it go. I love you forever and two days."

"One last question for you and I will never ask again. Are you sure you are ready to move to Aurora and be with me? No more hesitation on leaving your world behind?"

"None, I have found my mate and I have a feeling I have found some new best friends in Aurora. I know you will always keep me safe and I want to build a family with you right away. But tell me, what other surprises did you have for me before Bet'any ruined the fun?"

Quint growled and dropped his head on the pillow, "I had carolers set up to come and sing Earth Christmas songs for you, then we were going to go up into the mountains today and build a snowman, maybe have a snowball fight. I wanted to show you we could still do the same stuff here as you could on Earth."

Zaria sat up and looked into his eyes, happiness bloomed in her heart. "Thank you, that is the sweetest gift anyone could ever have given me. I'm sorry I called you Scrooge, you are the most giving man I have ever met."

"I don't remember you calling me Scrooge."

She grinned. "Not to your face, but I did."

"I forgive you, love," he kissed her and brushed the hair away from her sweaty face.

"What happened with Bet'any and the others?" She'd almost forgotten what brought them to the castle in the first place yesterday.

"There were only five people in this group, and no one had heard of them outside the small town. Viktor checked with the dragons, Talen the bears, Brecc with the wolves, no one was aware. Though to be safe, Karel sent out soldiers to the different shifter groups around Aurora to make sure there were not rumblings anywhere else. Alyx is taking care of the ones we caught, though the majority of shifters on Aurora are all for human mates. They know you have to sometimes look elsewhere to find your one love."

"Should someone let Gerri know? I mean she is setting up humans and shifters here. She may want to be notified there was a threat."

Alyx will take care of that, he speaks with her frequently. Quint rolled Zaria to her back. "Now what were you saying about cubs? I am ready to get started on our family if you are."

***

Zaria snuggled into her soft sweater and sipped on her hot cocoa. The snow flurries made her smile.

"You look like you came out of a postcard," Quint said from behind, curling his arms around her waist. "I'm surprised you're not wrapping things still."

"It's Christmas," she laughed. "I stopped wrapping and now all I get to do is enjoy the day. Oh, I made cookies."

"Ah, yes. That delightful scent had me up early." He kissed the side of her head and moved away. "I think I'll try them."

"You'll have to thank whoever you got to bring me the supplies so I could make us a nice dinner, including those."

"I'll let Alyx know. He had some brought for Bella and added ours to the list. She loves baking cookies for the kids."

She turned away from the beautiful falling flakes to watch Quint take a bite out of one of her cookies. "Do you like it?"

He winked. "Love it. Thankfully, I don't have to lie about these. They are really delicious."

She chuckled and shook her head, loving the comfy new sweater and sweats he'd gifted her. For a man who didn't like gifts, he'd gotten her the most beautiful things. Nothing crazy expensive, just thoughtful things she could use and loved. "Thanks. I'm excited to see the kids playing in the snow."

"We'll head to the town later, but first, I have to tell you something." He picked up a tiny box from under the tree, put it in his back pocket and headed her way. "You outdid yourself with the decorations. The house, the tree. Hell, even the trees outside."

She laughed at his shocked expression. "I had fun doing it. Bella and the other Earth girls loved helping. Then we went to each other's houses and did it again and again."

He shook his head and continued forward, stopping in front of her. "No wonder you were exhausted when you got home. And then you started wrapping gifts for the kids."

"And my new friends. I'm glad we were able to go back and get some things to help make this first Christmas special."

He raised a hand to her face, cupping her cheek. "You're beautiful. Your heart is amazing."

She warmed from the compliment and glanced away. "The people here are wonderful. And my new friends have made life so easy to love." She met his gaze again. "But you and all your hard work at making it easy for me to adjust. Getting me anything and everything to make the transition easier. You're the real amazing one."

He took a step back and lifted one of her hands to his lips. "Love does things to us. It makes us want to be that person that does whatever is necessary to prove we are worthy. I wanted to show you I am worthy of your love."

She nodded. "You did. You have it. My love. My heart. My soul. My everything."

"Good. Then maybe this part will be easier for you," he said and lowered down to one knee, reached into his back pocket and stared at her with an amount of love she never knew existed. "Will you marry me, Zaria?"

She blinked, her eyes stuck on his face and her brain processing the words. "What?"

He frowned. "I asked if you'd marry me. Were those the wrong words?"

She laughed and shook her head, her eyes watering from the humor and nerves.

"You won't marry me?"

More laughter escaped her. She blinked, trying not to mess up his moment. It was then she glanced at the open box displaying a beautiful ring. A ring unlike any she'd ever seen. It was an oval diamond with a halo, but the diamond was sparkling like a thousand stars were caught in it. "Those were the right words. And yes, I will marry you. I will, Quint."

He pulled up to both feet and kissed her. Her heart soared with happiness.

"Thank you, my love," he said, his arms going around her once he got the ring on her finger.

"This ring is just…wow. It's catching light from every angle. Like there's fireworks going off in it."

"I'm glad you like it."

She glanced at him. "Like it? I love it. But I thought we were mated. Isn't that marriage in the shifter world?"

He gave a quick nod. "Yes, but you're human. And I want marriage in your world. Besides, I heard all about wedding nights, and I have some ideas."

She laughed at the way he wagged his brows. "You pervert." Then she sighed and leaned into him, kissing his chin. "I love you, Quint."

"I love you, too, Zaria. Now let's go unwrap my present," he said, picking her up in his arms and carrying her to the bedroom.

EPILOGUE

Gerri sat back at her desk in her apartment on Earth, another satisfied shifter and his mate. With a smirk, Gerri thought about who was next. There were a few on Aurora she wanted to set up and a couple on Earth. Now it was time to figure out who was ready and up for the next challenge.

Maybe the lovely Juliet she'd met at her charity ball. She shivered. Juliet worked in that freezing cold. She needed someone to keep her warm. That would be a good one to find a man for. She really wanted her own happily ever after and was ready for it.

Maybe Dalissa was ready for a mate. That lioness was eager for a trip to Earth. A guide to show her around would be a perfect way to meet.

That would do nicely and it's a good idea to let Aurora handle their issues for a little bit before she traveled back there with a human by her side. One could never be too careful.

So many options, so little time.

The End…until next time

ABOUT THE AUTHOR

New York Times and USA Today Bestselling Author

Hi! I'm Milly Taiden. I love to write sexy stories featuring fun, sassy heroines with curves and growly alpha males with fur. My books are a great way to satisfy your craving for contemporary or paranormal romance with action, humor, suspense and happily ever afters.

I live in Florida with my hubby, our boys, and our fur children Speedy, Stormy and Teddy. I am seriously addicted to chocolate and cake.

I love to meet new readers, so come sign up for my newsletter and check out my Facebook page. We always have lots of fun stuff going on there.

SIGN UP FOR MILLY TAIDEN'S NEWSLETTER FOR LATEST NEWS, GIVEAWAYS, EXCERPTS, AND MORE!

http://eepurl.com/pt9q1

Find out more about Milly Taiden here:

Email: millytaiden@gmail.com
Website: http://www.millytaiden.com
Facebook:
http://www.facebook.com/millytaidenpage
Twitter: https://www.twitter.com/millytaiden

If you liked this story, you might also enjoy the following by Milly Taiden:

Sassy Mates / Sassy Ever After Series
Scent of a Mate *Book One*
A Mate's Bite *Book Two*
Unexpectedly Mated *Book Three*
A Sassy Wedding *Short 3.7*
The Mate Challenge *Book Four*
Sassy in Diapers *Short 4.3*
Fighting for Her Mate *Book Five*
A Fang in the Sass *Book 6*
Also, check out the **Sassy Ever After World on Amazon at** mtworldspress.com

A.L.F.A Series
Elemental Mating *Book One*
Mating Needs *Book Two*
Dangerous Mating *Book Three*
Fearless Mating *Book Four*

Savage Shifters
Savage Bite *Book One*
Savage Kiss *Book Two*
Savage Hunger *Book Three*
Savage Wedding *Book Four*

Drachen Mates
Bound in Flames *Book One*
Bound in Darkness *Book Two*

Bound in Eternity *Book Three*
Bound in Ashes *Book Four*

Federal Paranormal Unit
Wolf Protector *Federal Paranormal Unit Book One*
Dangerous Protector *Federal Paranormal Unit Book Two*
Unwanted Protector *Federal Paranormal Unit Book Three*

Paranormal Dating Agency
Twice the Growl *Book One*
Geek Bearing Gifts *Book Two*
The Purrfect Match *Book Three*
Curves 'Em Right *Book Four*
Tall, Dark and Panther *Book Five*
The Alion King *Book Six*
There's Snow Escape *Book Seven*
Scaling Her Dragon *Book Eight*
In the Roar *Book Nine*
Scrooge Me Hard *Short One*
Bearfoot and Pregnant *Book Ten*
All Kitten Aside *Book Eleven*
Oh My Roared *Book Twelve*
Piece of Tail *Book Thirteen*
Kiss My Asteroid *Book Fourteen*
Scrooge Me Again *Short Two*
Born with a Silver Moon *Book Fifteen*

Sun in the Oven *Book Sixteen*
Between Ice and Frost *Book Seventeen*
Book Eighteen (Coming Soon)

Also, check out the **Paranormal Dating Agency World on Amazon or at** mtworldspress.com

Raging Falls
Miss Taken *Book One*
Miss Matched *Book Two*
Miss Behaved *Book Three*
Miss Behaved *Book Three*
Miss Mated *Book Four*
Miss Conceived *Book Five (Coming Soon)*

FUR-ocious Lust - Bears
Fur-Bidden *Book One*
Fur-Gotten *Book Two*
Fur-Given Book *Three*

FUR-ocious Lust - Tigers
Stripe-Tease *Book Four*
Stripe-Search *Book Five*
Stripe-Club *Book Six*

Night and Day Ink

Bitten by Night *Book One*
Seduced by Days *Book Two*
Mated by Night *Book Three*
Taken by Night *Book Four*
Dragon Baby *Book Five*

Shifters Undercover
Bearly in Control *Book One*
Fur Fox's Sake *Book Two*

Black Meadow Pack
Sharp Change *Black Meadows Pack Book One*
Caged Heat *Black Meadows Pack Book Two*

Other Works
Wolf Fever
Fate's Wish
Wynter's Captive
Sinfully Naughty Vol. 1
Don't Drink and Hex
Hex Gone Wild
Hex and Kisses
Alpha Owned
Match Made in Hell
Alpha Geek

HOWLS Romances
The Wolf's Royal Baby

The Wolf's Bandit
Goldie and the Bears
Her Fairytale Wolf *Co-Written*
The Wolf's Dream Mate *Co-Written*
Her Winter Wolves *Co-Written*

Contemporary Works
Lucky Chase
Their Second Chance
Club Duo Boxed Set
A Hero's Pride
A Hero Scarred
A Hero for Sale
Wounded Soldiers Set

If you enjoyed the book, please consider leaving a review, even if it's only a line or two; it would make all the difference and would

Printed in Great Britain
by Amazon